THE SQUATTER

THE SQUATTER

A Novel-Memoir

by Ricardo R. Luna, Narrator &
Dr. Theophilus Ralph, Ghost Writer

SOL‿TION HOLE PRESS

SOL⏝TION HOLE PRESS

ISBN: 978-0-9981712-6-5 hard cover (Cloth-Blue)
ISBN: 978-0-9981712-7-2 soft cover (Perfect Bound)
ISBN: 978-0-9981712-8-9 ebook

Solution Hole Press LLC.
www.solutionholepress.com

Cover Design: Six Penny Graphics

Cover photos: © USM Photography/Adobe Stock.
© Ulia Koltyrina/Adobe Stock
Author's picture courtesy of Marie Safont Zurenda

FOR MARIE SAFONT ZURENDA,
kindred spirit, bibliobuddy, & fellow conspirator

PART 1

For those who might think the subject of this story to be metaphorical in nature, I fear disappointment may ensue. The "squatter" or "uninvited tenant" who has become the "other person inside your head" is in this particular case not a term to be applied to one's conscience, nor is it an alter ego, still less an incarnation of "voices" to be heard, like those that beset the religiously besotted—today we would say, the schizophrenic—Joan of Arc and induced her to commit actions she would not naturally have committed if she had only been left on her own. If I hear voices, they most assuredly don't tell me what to do. Besides, I hear only one voice, and all it wants is to converse with me. Every once in a while, it asks me for a favor, and he usually asks nicely.

What I do know is that this is a case of an embedded personality that came to me late in life. I am now pushing 60, or rather pulling it since it's from the other side. It made itself at home, and, without asking for my permission, began to share the inner space of my cranium, which subsequently became "our" cranium. I share space with a tenant who, for one reason or another, speaks directly with me "in thought," meaning silently, while we both are inside our head; but at other times this person insists on communicating with me externally, that is, he will write out notes for me on pieces of paper that I will be sure to run across, or through emails that he sends to me through the usual way. During those occasions of external communication, my personality, Ricardo R. Luna, is dormant, or asleep, or "out of it," and has no knowledge of the subject of such communication. When I read those slips of paper or emails for the first time, the message they convey comes as a complete surprise.

I believe that this other personality, Dr. Theophilus Ralph, is in control as to when we are in direct contact, during which time he conducts a completely normal conversation with me, although in our case it is silently, in other words, within our shared thoughts. But like I said, when we are separate and apart, he can decide to communicate with me through written texts. I do not, and cannot, control our mode of communication at all. He has his own volition and acts on his own, but since he doesn't drive, he frequently asks me to take him someplace.

When we communicate by thought conversation we are not limited to English. Dr. Ralph speaks German, although I don't. He speaks an excellent French, which I also know fluently. In addition, I speak Spanish, having been born in Guatemala; Dr. Ralph understands it a bit, but does not speak it.

The biggest biographical detail we share is that we both are, or in his case, was, a teacher of French, both of the language and of the literature. Apparently, he also taught history; I could, but at the college where I work I am not allowed to because I do not have enough post-graduate credits in the field. I'm an autodidact when it comes to history. Everything else between Dr. Ralph and me is a toss up. For instance, I am gay, but I have no idea what Dr. Ralph's sexuality is. He never speaks of men or women in a sexual way, unless we're speaking about characters in a novel, and I get the feeling that personally he is asexual. In case it's of any interest, whenever I am sexually engaged with my friend, Dr. Ralph manages to make himself scarce, even for hours afterwards. I don't know if he does this out of discretion, or out of lack of interest for the act, or because he is indeed titillated by what's going on but doesn't want me to know.

We can, and do, keep secrets from each other. He's the outsider, so there's tons of stuff I don't know about him. Everything I know is from what he tells me. But he's in my head all the time where he has felt free to rummage through everything about which I'm conscious. In experimentation, I have managed to succeed many times to keep him from knowing something by not thinking about it. This is hard to do but becomes better with practice. With most people, if you tell them not to think about something, they will think about it exclusively. There are some who are told not to discuss a subject, for one reason or another, but that's the first thing they'll blurt out when given the chance. Keeping a secret from Dr. Ralph is a lot like keeping a secret from a best friend or a lover. It can be sustained for quite a long time. Eventually, though, one's best friend or lover will find it out. Is it by your countenance, by the way you look away when a certain subject is broached, by your impatience to change the subject? Dr. Ralph, too, finds out my secrets, but I really don't care. My secrets are not deep or dark or threatening or self-incriminating. I lead a rather boring life, maybe even stultifying. I am a pretty normal college professor.

With the advent of my second personality, it could be argued, however, that I am normal no longer. But I must come to terms with the vocabulary. Is Dr. Ralph a second personality? Is he the evidence of what used to be called multiple personality disorder, and is now known as dissociative identity disorder? Most of the time I feel that he is just a second person, complete unto himself, who showed up one day on my threshold, inner threshold, that is, and simply crossed over inside my mind.

It didn't scare me. The first time he 'spoke' to me inside my head took place at the grocery store. He simply told me that the groceries I was purchasing were not conducive to my losing weight. This probably makes you think, of course, that this was the voice of my conscience speaking. But heretofore, my conscience never had a real voice, with authentic articulation and recognizable inflection. This was verifiable human language. It wasn't like a miniature angel sitting on my right shoulder looking out on everything I did and trying to manipulate me into doing the right thing, all the while counterbalancing the little devil installed on my left, or sinister, shoulder, shouting out to me to go for it! This was more discrete: I heard the voice, first of all, truly heard it, as if through my ears, and it was no metaphor. The voice's language was distinctly not figurative. It was real, it was clear, and he, a masculine voice, wasn't whispering or murmuring. It was as if someone were standing close to you on the aisle as you put your groceries on the checkout counter, saying, "You really think you should be buying those? Bo said that you were getting a paunch. Need I say more?" That was the exact statement the voice said.

I did not look around because I knew there was nobody there. By the way, did I mention that Dr. Ralph speaks with a slight German accent? I heard a distinctive voice which was not emanating from any external source, no real live person, no overhead speakers, no ear buds, no ventriloquist's antics. I simply put aside the chocolate power bars, cereal boxes and jar of Nutella and apologized to the clerk, saying that I had changed my mind about those items.

"No worries," answered the clerk. "I get the same craving for chocolate sometimes, but then I do some sit-ups and push-ups and—!" He made a gesture as if he were sweeping that craving right out of his mind.

I even offered to put back the displaced items but he again said, "No worries!" He said the bagboy would put them back.

Walking towards my car in the parking lot I expected to hear the voice again, but I didn't hear it for a few days. In the interim, I thought I had hallucinated the voice. I don't take drugs or pharmaceuticals, and keep alcohol to an acceptable minimum on the weekends, so I knew that these weren't the culprit on a Thursday afternoon. It happened that first time, but I knew, or rather, I felt, that it would happen again.

I was right. On the following Sunday, as I was gardening a bit reluctantly, since it was a drizzly day, my voice said to me, "Go inside, why don't you? It's not a nice day for gardening. Shouldn't you be on your novel working?"

I placed my gardening tools next to the flowers I had just planted.

"How do you know I'm working on a novel?"

"It was clear as day. I saw the file when you went in to change a couple of words. I like the title, by the way."

"What title is that? I've changed it so many times."

"The file read *Dr. Jekyll and Mr. Hyde Travel to France*."

"That's not my novel. That's a piece that I'm working on for a literary magazine. It's on the influence of Robert Louis Stevenson on Ionesco's play *Rhinocéros*."

"Ah, I see."

"The name of my novel is *The Many Lives of Webster Buchanan*."

"Are you okay?" asked an external voice that jolted me out of my reverie. It was Bo who had come out of the house. "You've been kneeling in front of those flowers for such a long time, and it's started to rain harder. It's like you've hardly noticed. You're soaked. Shouldn't you come in?"

I looked at one of my shoulders and saw that I was indeed soaked.

"I was thinking," I answered. "I was in a different world."

"Well, come back to this one. The flowers can wait."

I wanted to say, "The flowers are already planted," but it was easier just to follow Bo back into the house. Dr. Ralph, or rather, my mysterious internal voice, seemed not to have come back with me, for I didn't hear from him for another few days. Mind, at that time I still didn't know what his name was. I suppose that proper introductions weren't made until the third time I heard from the voice inside my head.

It was in the morning as soon as I had woken up, before my coffee, just at the time when I require absolute silence and tranquility, or else I become an untameable Mr. Hyde.

The voice spoke but I was still so sleepy that the words seemed unintelligible. I hadn't even been able to register the language in which they had been spoken, that sort of thing.

"Please do me a favor?" repeated the voice in his usual French.

"A favor? What is this? It's so early in the morning! I haven't had my coffee. Whatever it is, it can wait till I have my coffee."

Utter silence reigned until I went into the kitchen, prepared a full carafe for myself, sat down while I waited for the coffee to filter, then took a full mug to the kitchen table. Only when I had finished half of my first mug of the morning did the voice speak anew.

"You are so grumpy when you wake up. I apologize for bothering you."

I interrupted the reading of the news on my iPad. "Well, what is it? But first, who are you, and what are you doing inside my head?"

"My name is Theophilus Ralph, I am an historiographer and professor of linguistics and European literatures. I was in Westphalia born. I don't know what I am doing inside your head, if that is indeed where I am. All I know is that I woke up here, and I am no longer at home, no longer doing the things that I've always been doing. I realize that I'm no longer in control of my own life, which bothers me a great deal, and I miss being home, and I miss being me, or just me. I know who you are, from what I've been able to gather. I'm not always awake here, and sometimes time goes by, hours, perhaps days at a stretch. It must be that I still need to sleep every once in a while. I have been waking up here for quite some time, maybe a few weeks. I didn't realize that I could so easily with you communicate. When you were at the grocery store I saw that you were making a mistake, buying fattening foods. That's why I spoke. I couldn't help it. I see you have a weak will."

"There is nothing wrong with my will. I just like chocolate, and, frankly, I can't live without it. I'd rather be fat."

"But Bo said—"

"What do you know of Bo? I'm not sure I like you eavesdropping on my conversations with Bo. What do I do to get my privacy back?"

"I don't know. I don't know how this happened. I don't want to pry into your affairs, but I can't help it. I'm living here now, and I see things, I hear things. The same things you see and hear. But I can't feel your personal things. Inside. I mean, I can feel when you touch something cold or hot, but I can't feel your feelings. I can only surmise them from how you react, how you go about living your daily life. Just like it is with another person. For instance, I can surmise that you love Bo very much, that he is important in your life, and I feel that you should hearken to his words."

"Hearken to his words? What kind of French is that? And why do you have a German accent? Of all people to have barging in on me, why did it have to be a German?"

"Why, do you have something against Germans?"

"Well, yes, yes—I do, yes! Look at all those messes you started, and I'm not just talking about World Wars I and II. Those are just what the common people remember. I remember farther back, like the Paris Commune in 1871, and the Polish Partition of 1772, and the Seven Years' War, with Frederick II, what was so 'Great' about that? Germans have been stepping on other people's toes for three centuries. You feel that you can just encroach on other people's sovereignty without compunction, just take over what you covet. You want Silesia, just take it. You want Pomerania, just move right on in. A big chunk of Poland, make yourself at home. Half the civilized world, why not, it's yours!"

My spluttering came to a stop and I tipped the mug to get the last gulp. I'm telling you, in the morning I am a beast.

"I suppose that you are right," said Theophilus Ralph. "But I can't for the actions of generations of my compatriots apologize. They were responsible for what they did; I am responsible for what I do."

After a few moments, he added, "You got stuck with a German inside your head; I'm forced to live in Miami."

I made a face, which he couldn't see. I was at the kitchen counter pouring myself another full mug of coffee.

"You're going to get jittery with that," said the stupid voice.

Ignoring it would certainly transmit my anger, and I pretended I was all alone in the kitchen. As a matter of fact, I thought of calling Bo and making a date for lunch that afternoon.

Which I did, uninterruptedly. Bo was pleasantly surprised, and we agreed to meet for lunch at Bayside, since it was equidistant from my college and his medical building.

I didn't hear from Ralph for about a week. Only afterwards did I remember that he had been asking me for a favor when we were in the kitchen. What that favor was I had no clue.

During the week I perused the possibilities of the sudden onset of a voice inside my head: I was going crazy; I was… I was going crazy. What the…? What other explanation could I have found? There were no possibilities in the plural. There was only one conclusion to make. As both a literary and a scientific person, I could visit the world of literature and science where I could delve into other explanations, none of which I truly found satisfactory, at least not for my particular case. Was this voice a ghost? Was he an aural specter? Was he an anomaly of the space-time continuum? Was he an intelligence who had lost his body, along with his physical mind? Was he an extraterrestrial? Posing as a German? And how did he come to me? By transmission? Transcendent reverie? Telepathy? Telekinesis? Teleportation? Telegraphic extension? Telematics? Telesthesia? Contagion? Protoplasmic projection? Hypnotic suggestion? Double soul exposure? Random personality duplication? Cognitive facsimile replication?

What did these things even mean? Another person, a stranger and a foreigner, somehow muscled his way into my head and all of a sudden my psyche was doubled. Why I didn't doubt my own sanity from the very beginning of this intrusion is still a mystery to me. Perhaps it is because my whole life I have detected that my hold on reality has been rather tenuous; when pondering the writings of those authors and poets who were considered to be loopy, I felt kinships with them. Gérard de Nerval is still one of my favorite poets. As he walked his pet lobster down Parisian streets he saw and heard—imagined?— packs of wild dogs terrorizing the neighborhoods. I could deal with that. My favorite raconteur, Guy de Maupassant, in his story *Le Horla,* introduces a protagonist who believes he is possessed, haunted, by a malevolent being. My immediate reaction is to empathize with him! My lack of affinity for stable mental health prepared me, I think, for my external voice, my otherworldly voice, my outlandish voice. Literature also prepared me for the peculiar, the unfamiliar, the astounding, the unexpected. The ghost in Charlotte Brontë's *Villette*: I was so disappointed to find out it wasn't a ghost. The heroine had accepted it as a ghost, and didn't ask any questions about it. It is absolutely normal to see a ghost in the attic. And didn't it brush against her as it fled from the room? She *saw* it, then she *felt* it.

Another reason why I say that my hold on reality does not have that much tensile strength is the feeling I sometimes get that my being alive is spurious. While most of the time I do feel alive and know that my blood runs through my veins, that my senses are picking everything up the way they should, every once in a while I feel that I'm a dream. Mind, it's not that I am in a dream. I look out at the world and feel that I *am* the dream, a dream dreamt by someone else. Sometimes this becomes the idea that I am a character in a story written by somebody else. I look out at life and the sight seems to be scenery propped up for a play, including clouds overhead and breezes controlled by huge fans offstage flowing through the attached branches of ersatz trees.

Just in case, I did read up on schizophrenia. What a messed-up disorder that one is! But that was it, I felt I wasn't messed up. Listen, I'm not stupid. I realize that feelings of normalcy are the wacko's way, excuse me, the patient's way of avoiding the acceptance of reality, but I was convinced that, other than the one voice that I could hear in my head, I had no other symptoms, no other faulty perceptions, and certainly no withdrawal from reality to facilitate the plunge into a world of fantasy and delusion. I still felt whole, that I myself was still whole; none of me was missing, no fragmentation of my psychological configuration had taken place. I was still me, complete with my memories, my desires, my volition, my habits, my idiosyncrasies, and, as far as I could tell, my wits.

I suppose that it did take me a while to accept the premise that I am no longer alone. Perhaps I shall never be alone again. I am accompanied in life now, everywhere I go, in everything I do. As a matter of fact, now I do things and go places I never would have done or gone, simply because this other anima within me asks me to do him the favor.

The favor Dr. Ralph had wanted to ask me that morning in my kitchen was to take him to the Salvador Dalí Museum in St. Petersburg. It was no big deal. There's a bookstore I like to visit in Tampa, so, two birds with one stone, I took him there. I even invited Bo to come along.

I need to convince you that Dr. Ralph is a nice guy. He does not press me to do the favors he asks of me. He is polite, and sometimes he must accept my final decision if it's a negative. He tried mightily to get me to fly to Regensburg on my last vacation. But I already had plans to go to Paris and Normandy with my friend Bo. I told Dr. Ralph that Regensburg would have to wait. He's still waiting, but he still wants to go. Maybe next year. There is a convention in Munich I wouldn't mind going to, on medieval literature.

This reminds me: Are there any advantages at all in this intrusion of another person inside my head? Absolutely. In class, for instance, I am now double the teacher I used to be. I have my own education, of course, via the University of Miami, then Rutgers for my doctoral work, but I find myself augmented by this whole other education that I get from Dr. Ralph, and which I am convinced comes from Europe. His knowledge of French medieval literature is greater than mine. I studied more than the minimum required courses at Rutgers, but Dr. Ralph must have taken supplementary workshops on the period. For instance, I always teach the usual poets of the Middle Ages, such as Bernard de Ventadour, and I include in the reading material several of his better known poems, especially his *cansos,* or poems on the subject of love. Dr. Ralph takes this several steps further. He knows about the *contrafacta* that were made of Ventadour's *cansos.* A *contrafactum* is a duplication of sorts where another poet-composer takes a well-known love song, borrows its melodic line and places instead a text of his own making. This is not completely unknown in recent times with people like "Weird Al" Yankovic taking a song by Michael Jackson or Madonna and splicing his own words onto the melody. In any case, here was Dr. Ralph in the middle of class humming to me the *canso Can vei la lauzeta mover* with its matching *contrafactum*! I refused to transliterate him and his music to my students.[1] Not until we could practice it at home, I told him. He agreed. The following session I presented the full extended lesson to my students, how certain songs were copied and imitated, how certain melodies were instantaneously recognizable, and how the new composition gained in its intertextual and intermelodical blending.

---

[1] I use the word 'transliterate' instead of 'translate' or 'interpret' because transliteration entails coming up with corresponding symbols in a homologous language. Conveying the message of the voice of Dr. Ralph is tantamount to describing a dream, in other words, going from what is intrinsically understood to something that another person will understand.

Bo has now become a third wheel in these psychological, teleological transmutations. I say psychological with trepidation; but teleological makes more sense: how to explain the design and purpose of my material mind that now housed two entities? I was driving the two entities to St. Petersburg and Tampa, plus Bo in the passenger seat beside me. But he had no inkling as to what was going on inside my mind. I thought it might be fun to share my anomalous squatter with him, but knowing that he was a medical doctor threw a hypothetical wrench in my musings. Even though he would be in a superior position to comprehend my situation, he might be the first to disparage it as mere illusions, visions with an underlying physical, or worse, psychotic, cause. Doctors have a way of dismissing factual matters that conflict with what they have learned, like my cardiologist pshawing at my comment that I could detect the onset of my left bundle branch block and also its departure. Instead of coming with me to Florida's west coast, Bo, or rather, Dr. Solomon, would direct me to the nearest psychiatric hospital. Doctors educated in the west rely too heavily on rational, commonsensical analyses. Paranormal occurrences are anathema to them. Everything is weighed and measured with scientific rigor. I was afraid Bo would think me a fruitcake. We went all the way to Tampa with Bo still steeped in complete ignorance. Luckily Dr. Ralph didn't speak to me on the way there. But once there at the museum, he came alive and sprang up from within me in quite an energetic and loquacious mood. He couldn't stop jabbering.

Take me to this painting, now take me to that one, and the other one over there, and, wait, are we forgetting, no, there it is, it's in that next room…

I was both guide and proxy, for I was the one who had to ask questions of the museum staff when searching for a particular painting. There was one that I believe was the reason why we went to the Dalí Museum in the first place. Dr. Ralph became completely silent when we found *Slave Market with the Disappearing Bust of Voltaire*. It is an arresting piece, a devious and masterful trompe l'œil, as the mind sees the two Spanish women from the Edad de Oro who give way to the grinning head of Voltaire and then back to the two women.

We stood in front of this piece for so long that finally Bo said, "What is it you like about this painting?"

Both Dr. Ralph and I answered at the same time, although Bo could only hear my answer. "Because I've always loved trompe l'œil, just as I like optical illusions, for the tricks of deception that the eye cannot fathom. Our brain does not allow us to see the two images, the women and Voltaire's head, at the same time. It's either one or the other, consecutively, not simultaneously. It's proof that we are incapable of exact observation, and that's why a lot of science escapes us. We cannot see, we cannot sense, what is obvious to other creatures with better, broader senses. We need technical stand-ins, telescopes and microscopes, chronoscopes and chromoscopes, galvanoscopes, thermoscopes and hygroscopes. We also need go-betweens like robotic probes who visit planets that cannot sustain us, and who do the interpreting for us. Left on our own, we cannot interpret very well."

Bo seemed impressed.

Dr. Ralph's answer was not as long, so I repeated it to Bo,

"I also suspect that Dalí disapproves of Voltaire."

"How so?" asked Bo.

Since I didn't know, I had to wait until Dr. Ralph furnished the answer. "Because the whole world of rational skepticism, which Voltaire represents, becomes precarious in a slave market. Actually, it's ejected, uhm, I mean *re*jected. Dalí is suggesting that rationalism is for sale, too, as an investment. You can buy it, you can use it, put it away for a rainy day, but in the end, it is just like any other speculation. And when it gets older and loses its teeth you need another slave."

Bo looked at me and said in amazement, "What?"

"Wait a minute, wait a minute. It's a stretch but it makes sense to me."

"I hope it does since you're the one saying it."

"Uh, well, yes, but think about it. Rationalism is just a commodity like anything else. It has value that rises or falls through time. Romanticism had no use for it; industrialism extolled it; surrealism thought it pretty valueless; existentialism thought of it as one more ridiculous thing valued by the bourgeoisie. You use it if you believe in it, you dislodge it from your portfolio if you see something else that catches your eye."

"Why are you speaking in such a halting manner?"

"Sometimes I need to collect my thoughts. Besides, Voltaire is staring at me. I for one always appreciated the man."

"Wasn't he an atheist?"

"But he spent his whole life for God looking!"

"What?"

"I mean, looking for God. Looking for God."

"Let's go have lunch."

It was a mistake to transliterate Dr. Ralph in real time. Even language interpreters need time to formulate their translations.

Listening to a voice and transmitting its message is not easy. Try it the next time you are listening to the news. Repeat out loud exactly what you are hearing, and see if you can catch your breath. Then imagine that you are translating into another language at the same time.

After lunch we visited more of the museum, but right before we left, Dr. Ralph wanted one more minute in front of *The Slave Market*. He was obsessed, and in a way, he "contaged" me; not just because of his proximity to me, namely, zero centimeters, but also because he was using my senses, and my senses were beginning to adapt to his way of thinking. I really didn't mind. My senses still work pretty well: lately I need glasses to read but not for long distance. My ears are better than most (I am still the first to hear a water leak someplace in the house, even in one not my own). Everything else is doing okay. I have enough senses for two people.

Oh, a detail: I inherited from my mother the so-called sex-linked trait of daltonism. I am color-blind. Apparently, Dr. Ralph was not. He says my world is lackluster and gray. But I see enough colors to think the world beautiful. I can see the jacarandas and tabebuias in bloom, for their flowers are lilac and yellow, respectively; I cannot see the poincianas or hibiscus in bloom, with their red and orange flowers.

I was, of course, born alone. No twin. I came into this world in 1955 at the following coordinates, 14.6284° N, 90.5227° W, which makes it smack in the middle of Guatemala City, six blocks away from the National Palace. When I was four, my parents moved to the States, to Dade County, Florida, as a matter of fact. Ironically, they were moving to the country that had made them want to move out of Guatemala in the first place. The "bloodless" coup d'état staged by the CIA in 1954 was not completely without violence. My mother tells the story of how soldiers with machine guns burst into the National Palace to oust everybody who had been working for the current administration. Her uncle was Minister of Education but she worked as a secretary in a different department of the Palace. That was the last day she and her colleagues worked there. Under the stare of heavily armed soldiers, all the employees filed out carrying only their personal belongings. Everything else, letters still in typewriters, files in the interdepartmental mailboxes, messages coming out of the telex machines, forgotten sandwiches in refrigerators, all of that was left behind. The new residents of the palace came a few hours later and claimed everything for themselves. The new occupiers made themselves at home and refurbished the place in delicate guerrilla pastels of green, light brown and cream.

My parents already had a first child, a girl. With the advent of the sister who followed me, they decided to bolt. Guatemala was not a good place to raise children. If our family stayed there, the children would learn about the forcible overthrow of governments and Communist uprisings and counter-revolutionary terrorism. Two of my uncles, Mario López Villatoro and Francisco Curley García were murdered in the streets as they went about their daily business, Mario by leftist extremists in a busy shopping mall in Guatemala City, surrounded by his children, Francisco by rightist death squads in his native Alta Verapaz. My parents wanted their children to learn about social stability and the peaceable transmission of governmental power and the secure establishment of rules and regulations and checks and balances of a well-ordered nation with a strong, unfaltering constitution. We moved to Hialeah in February of 1959 where we were the only Latins around.

We spoke Spanish at home, I learned English in school, but in high school I learned the language that I wanted to choose for myself, the one I loved the most: French. I never felt that I made a special effort to learn this most beautiful and fascinating language. Rather, it was as if I came home to it. It was a return to the tongue of my avatars and it felt so comfortable and so… so… so fitting. The way you fit in your favorite bergère.

Between high school and college I came out of the closet, went through the usual and customary period of strife and stress, but after all was done, the new me emerged like from a chrysalis, much happier, more self-possessed, definitely more confident in what I wanted to do in life. Gone were my studies of architecture, for that is what my father had wanted of me, and in their stead came years and years—I wish they could have continued!—of studies of French literature, where I felt at home, where the readings were demanding but stimulating, and which, in the end, gave me a profession of which I was proud. Teaching French language and literature to 18-year-old students from the Americas was not easy, but it was dignified and fulfilling. My father grew to be proud of me as well. My sisters became architects.

I loved to blow up my pupils' balloons. The Haitians came in with an automatic defense mechanism that did not allow for perusals of other faiths. Many of them, Protestants, were convinced that Catholics were not even Christians, or at least, not true Christians. The Christian Bible was, of course, sacrosanct and legitimate. I sarcastically told them that I agreed, and that I had therefore decided to imitate the superlative lives of Abraham and Solomon. I wished to return to that bold and honest-to-goodness life of having multiple wives and possessing slaves. If some of my wives got too old to have children, I would get new ones, younger and sturdier, who would give me many, many sons. And who couldn't do with a few slaves to help around the house and in the garden? Not too many, I said, just a few. I had plenty of room in my back yard to pitch some tents where they could live. That last detail especially got their eyes to goggle and their jaws to drop, since they were Haitians living in Miami. They had so quickly adapted to air conditioning.

For the Cubans I had some pithy comments to get them to soften their anti-Communist, anti-Socialist stance. I would tell them that they should be proud of what their country had accomplished in just one generation: they had the highest literacy rate in the hemisphere, beating even the Americans! And their rums and cigars were the best in the world. Who needed sugar? Just get the whole country to produce rum and cigars and their economic woes would be over. During depressions and recessions people keep drinking, and Cuba libres are indeed very popular with the Spring Break crowds. When Cuba was *libre* we would all meet in Havana and celebrate. But the Cubans in Miami were not amused. They wanted to suffer and stew in their cold schemes of revenge. As impotent as they were in their actions, their minds were wonderfully full of intricate machinations of overthrowing those who had usurped them. I could understand; nobody likes to be usurped.

Least of all me. Not that Dr. Ralph had seized possession of me in totality. I was still free to pursue the fancies and caprices of my volition, and I did. But Dr. Ralph was like a bud on a graft, sitting on my psyche, borrowing my senses in order to look out into the world, and constantly reminding me of his existence. I say constantly, in reality it was more like occasionally, perhaps at times sporadically. He seldom bothered me. He stopped coming to me in the mornings. He learned I was a monster and would bite his head off. I need to be alone, in silence, in subdued light, in the morning. He learned that the earliest he could come into communication with me was during my commute to work, although he knew very well that he would be interrupting one of my Books on Tape. But if it was pressing enough, he would shoulder his way through. One time when I was reading, or rather, listening to Defoe's *The Plague Year*, he interjected with an excited voice, "Rick, look! Look over there, eleven o'clock."

Just past the toll in Cutler Ridge, where the turnpike rises to form an artificial hill, I saw two elongated rotating dark-gray ribbons dancing and winding down from the sky, and at the moment I looked, one of them stretched to meet the ground. A cloud of dust and debris rose around the point of impact. My heart raced when I realized it had struck buildings. I was horrified but could not even slow down. If you slow down on the turnpike in Miami you have a row of very unhappy people who feel free to exact revenge. So as I careened forward with the traffic streaming around me and behind me, all I could do was flow on and continue to watch the twin twisters as the second one hit the ground as well.

Was no one else watching this? At that point past Cutler Ridge, the turnpike jogs to the north-east, and the twisters were due north. By this time, they were at ten o'clock, then nine, but most drivers were still applying make-up and texting their co-workers so their eyes where on their rear-view mirror or down to their phone save for an occasional glance at the car right in front of them. I myself had been so ensconced in 17th-century London that I would not have perceived the tornadoes had it not been for my passenger's keen vision.

That's when I learned that Dr. Ralph was indeed autonomous, and that his mind could see out of my eyes independently of me. I was so unnerved by the tornadoes that I said nothing to Dr. Ralph. Only later did I realize that I should have thanked him, but then again, perhaps not. Who wants to see such a terrible sight on the commute to work in the morning? I think I would have preferred not to. In the news that evening one of the homeowners hit by the tornado was interviewed in front of his demolished home. He had been at work when the tornado hit and nobody had been inside the house. He explained that he had just finished with the repairs to the damage caused by a waterspout that had formed over one of the numerous lakes around his home, traveled up a street to strike only his home. I hoped that he had a provision in his insurance policy for double indemnity.

S lowly I began to piece together biographical information about Dr. Ralph, or at least, pieces of it. Dr. Ralph is a very private person. He doesn't dislodge much about his past. I was able to find out that Dr. Ralph is a Gemini, as am I. Only he's from the front end, and I'm from the back, his birthday being May 30th and mine June 17th. When I told him that his birthday was also the date of Voltaire's death, in 1778, he seemed not to be interested. He told me that my birthday fell on Iceland's Independence Day, only it was in 1944. I found it fascinating, especially since I love three authors who have connections to Iceland, Jules Verne, whose novel *Voyage to the Center of the Earth* begins in Snæfellsnes, the peninsula in western Iceland on which lies a dormant volcano, entry into the netherworld; Pierre Louÿs, a French novelist who wrote *Icelandic Fisherman*, and Halldór Laxness, the Icelandic novelist who won the Nobel Prize for literature in 1955, the year of my birth. I told Dr. Ralph that I loved having a personal connection with Iceland. I also liked the Vikings very much and Viking literature, not necessarily for their marauding and pillaging, but for their interesting sagas and clever myths. I would also like to believe in little people, furtive elves and trolls who live amidst the glens and meadows, ready to trip up an unsuspecting passerby.

Other than his birthday I have found out the following details about Dr. Ralph:

He's from Westphalia, Germany, but he used to live in Regensburg, hence his desire to travel there.

He has been a professor for many, many years, first of history, then of European literatures.

He is married, so I doubt he's gay. He loves his wife very much. He refuses to say anything about her, except that she's very beautiful. Oh, and she's French. He considers himself very lucky to have such a beautiful wife, when he himself is not that handsome.

He considers himself ugly. He thinks I'm very handsome, I suppose because I'm the Latin type, with thick hair that is still mostly black and hangs down to my shoulders and about my eyes. Bo prefers me with longish hair. What can I say, we are children of the 60s. Dr. Ralph was short and fat; I'm tall and fat. But there are still muscles underneath the fat. The last descriptor comes from Bo, who is rail-thin and preaches that if

I lost weight I would be off the high blood pressure and high cholesterol pills. I point out to him that he's on them. He responds that his body and background are different. He's Jewish. He tells me that I'm part Maya. I tell him that there's no proof of that; my ancestors were all white European. He answers that there's no way a Spanish family could have lived in Central America for two hundred years without Mayan blood infiltrating in. To shut him up I'll have to take one of those genetic tests to see where I do come from. Perhaps I am part Maya. I think, the more the merrier. Makes for a stronger, sturdier organism. Maybe I'm a reverter back to the original species, homo erectus. Bo says he believes it. I bop him on the nose. Things get out of control and we wrestle and roughhouse, ending up falling in bed where a different set of activities replaces the grappling, or rather changes its tenor. Dr. Ralph disappears and is forgotten.

D r. Ralph began to ask me about Bo and my relationship with him, interrogating me about where we met, how long we've been together, that sort of thing. I answered his questions. He was not the first straight person I had come across who was curious about gay relationships. I told him Bo and I met at Uncle Charlie's twenty-two years ago, on a Good Friday, and since then we've celebrated our anniversary on Good Friday rather than on the calendar date. It's easier to do it that way for we can't forget. Dr. Ralph asks if Bo's family came to the States during the Nazi invasion of France.

"Why do you think he's French?" I asked.

"Well, his name is Beau."

Since we were think-speaking in French I realized he was misspelling Bo's name. "No, his name is not b-e-a-u; it's Bo, b-o, short for Boaz, the man who rescued Ruth and then married her."

"Are you married to him?"

"No. We're allowed to now, but we both think that marriage is anachronistic and unnecessary. But I'm glad we've been given the choice. We're now treated, almost, like equal citizens."

"It must be tough for Bo to be both Jewish and gay."

"Why do you say that? Because you harbor prejudices against both?"

"No, no, of course not. I agree that gays should be treated equally in society. Germany had its heyday of gay toleration way before America. Read Christopher Isherwood!"

"Yes, and I also read Proust and André Gide. They were 'tolerated' up to a point but a lot of their writing is veiled and cryptic: you needed to know the key to understand the clues. I was 19 years old the first time I read Gide's *Corydon*. I hardly understood what he was talking about! This wasn't a gay manifesto; it was a pseudo-scientific treatise on homosexuality in animals. It sure was a big leap to get to humans. Today, Gide could be a lot more straightforward and liberate his text from the shadows in which he was accustomed to lurk. I think he finally discovers the freedom he sought in the sun of Africa: there he could cavort in freedom with the whole lit-up sky as witness, with no one around to be judgmental."

"Now you are being cryptic. What do you mean by 'cavort'?"

"I mean that he was free to, to..., to have sex with young men out in the open."

"You see, it's still difficult to mention that little word, 'sex'!

I'm surprised you didn't use the euphemism 'to make love'!"

"Well, no, I don't think there was love to it. I'm sure Gide was fond of the fellows he met in Africa, but, I think it was just the physical thing he was after."

"You love Bo, don't you? I feel it, since I'm living so close to you."

"Well, yes. From the very first moment I saw him, at Uncle Charlie's. It was a bar on Bird Road. Today it's a used-car lot. The light from above lit up his hair so that it looked like a halo."

"Oh, it was a hagiographic moment. I love those!"

"I didn't think he was a saint, for Pete's sake. It's just that his head looked so beautiful, so calm and self-assured. He asked me if the guy who had just left me was my boyfriend. I blurted out, 'No, he isn't! He's just someone I know.' And from that moment on we were together. It was so simple, so dramatic, so, so... unchallengeable! I've loved him from that first day and not once have I even thought of the possibility of making love to somebody else. I, who thought that faithfulness in a gay relationship was not just impossible but unnecessary, I've had to change my mind."

"I think that's beautiful," said Dr. Ralph. "Very beautiful indeed."

Then he must have left for I said something else, but he didn't answer back.

One day Dr. Ralph grumbled about living in Miami. This is how he put it: "When I first read Camus' *The Plague* I thought, who lives in Oran? What a weird place to live, at the tip of the desert, it's so hot and dry. About Miami, I say, who lives there, at the tip of the swamp? It's so hot and muggy. No four seasons. Just hot and hotter. No mountains, everything is flat as far as the eye can see. No rivers, save for the Miami River that looks no different than the hundreds of canals, only with more twists and turns. No cultural activities of any kind. Just modern art shows and modern music concerts. It is all art and music that will certainly not withstand the test of time. Miami itself won't withstand the test of time. All it will take is a well-directed hurricane and it will all be swept out to Biscayne Bay. No more city, just swamp once more."

I responded in defense of the city in which I grew up. "Well, there's the people. The people are vibrant and appealing. They come from everywhere, from everywhere in the world. You hear all sorts of languages on the streets and in the restaurants. Our restaurants are among the best in the world. Trump has a presence here. Ricky Martin lives here, and the Estefans. Alex Rodriguez, Alonzo Mourning. So does José José."

"Except for Trump, who are those people? I only know about Trump, and you should be ashamed to have him in your midst."

"Well, he doesn't actually live here. He just has real estate here."

I could see how a foreigner was disappointed to have to spend time in Miami. I lived in the outskirts, in a small village called Princeton, where the poor immigrants used to live before Andrew. Well, their ramshackle homes were the first ones to be wiped out. The official tally of dead in the wake of Andrew was risibly short of the truth: the government officials never counted the dead immigrants! In any case, it took me an hour to get to my college in downtown Miami. I went through Goulds, Cutler Ridge, Perrine, Palmetto Bay, Pinecrest, South Miami, Coral Gables, Little Havana and finally downtown. It was all a cultural desert, save for a few neighborhood theaters in the Gables and Little Havana.

I didn't even mention the beaches to Dr. Ralph. It had been so long since I had been to one, I didn't even remember if they were beautiful. Forget the Beach, Miami Beach. Once you crossed Biscayne Bay you were in a different world, one in which the young and the restless and the homicidal lived. How two cities, Miami and Miami Beach, could live side by side like that was beyond comprehension. The only place I liked was the neighborhood in-between, on the Venetian Causeway, with it's old Florida houses and old-time style. The revivified flair of Art Deco in the Beach seemed overreaching, anachronistic and oh so fake.

I have no copyright of my personality: another can come and share my inner space. I don't hold a grudge against Dr. Ralph who one day showed up inside my head. It was not of his own doing, it was not his fault, and he is not responsible. Of this I am certain. He told me it was a complete surprise to him when he woke up conscious inside me. At the beginning he lay low while he reconnoitered his new surroundings. It was as if he were crouching, hiding inside my mind, not willing to see out of my eyes and hear out of my ears. He says he spent a lot of time sleeping. He believes that sleep is when the brain, or the mind, or whatever the heck we have inside our skull, excuses itself from life for a few hours to be able to make sense of it all. Sleep is when you piece things together, when you get some understanding of the photons and the airwaves and the molecules, all the different ways that nature has to transmit its messages to us. Without these we would be blind, deaf, unable to smell, taste or feel. The body has to stop the barrage for a few hours while the mind resolves the messages and interprets them for us. Without sleep we go mad, they say. Well, Dr. Ralph thought at first he had gone mad, then with the passage of time he realized he was involved with someone. He could still remember his life, the things he used to do when he lived in Regensburg. He remembered details such as living on the same street where Johannes Kepler espied the other planets through his telescope.

I asked him to tell me the last thing he could remember.

"It's such a jumble," he answered. "You are asking me to remember what happened the most recently, say a few months ago, maybe even a few weeks. But I don't remember. I just don't remember."

Together we Googled him. He had an article, but no picture, mostly for the books he published, all of them in Germany, although one of them was translated into English: *The War of the Gods, from Roncesvalles to New York,* published in 2007 by the University Presses of Thunder-den-Drang. It was out of print through Amazon and Barnes & Noble, so I made a mental note to order it through AbeBooks. It looked interesting. It was about the internecine struggles between the world's great religions. Even though they all promised peace, they sure as hell visited chaos and conflict upon the others. This was one of the reasons that I decided to step away from the fray and become an atheist. Such freedom I felt, such relief. No more wasted time and effort to make sense of the nonsensical, to instill meaning in the meaningless, to eke out reasons for the irrational. So here was another reason why Dr. Ralph and I were compatible.

When I was alone, or at least, thought I was alone, I sort of came up with the theory that Dr. Ralph had died, or rather, his mortal body had died, but his mind had not. Mind, by the way, the French call *esprit,* so perhaps his spirit did not die along with his biological survival unit. Somehow his spirit flew from Regensburg to Miami and got into my mind. Or perhaps it happened when I was closer to Regensburg, when I went on a vacation to France. I was mostly in Normandy, but I got as far east as Savoy with this last trip I took. Maybe it happened then, and I picked him up like a traveler picks up an infection while abroad. I didn't pick up malaria or sleeping sickness from the tsetse fly, not even the flu. But I certainly picked up Dr. Ralph!

What happened to him and how did he get to me?

These were the two questions that pestered us. By Jove, I was willing to find out. As impatient as I was to ask him questions, I had to wait until he next got in touch with me. I have never been able to conjure him forth, another reason why I don't think he is my multiple personality. When he did contact me I told him that I wanted to find out what had happened to him and how he had shown up at my doorstep, my mind's doorstep.

"How do you propose we do this? We might have to travel to Regensburg, talk to my family, talk to my coworkers."

"Before we go gallivanting off during my semester, let's try something easier. Let's use Skype!"

"What's that?"

"It's used to make international calls through the computer. It can't be that difficult to call your department and find out."

"I wish I had thought of that," he answered.

"Let's do it, yes?"

After a moment's hesitation, he said, "All right."

We left this project for early the following morning because of the time difference. As soon as I had my required coffee in me, I went to my Mac and woke it up.

"All right, Ralph, are you there?" (I had started calling him Ralph because it sounded more friendly. We had also started using the *tu* form with each other in French, rather than the formal *vous* with which we had started. After all, we were sharing the same skull. We had a right to call each other familiar.)

"Awake and ship-shape!" was his answer.

Jeez! It was still too early in the morning for his vim.

"All right," I said, trying to sound positive while maneuvering my mouse to Google. "What is the name of your university?"

When there was no answer after a few seconds I asked, "Ralph, you still there?"

"Yes, I'm here, but for the life of me I don't remember. I just don't remember."

"That's okay," I commiserated. "All right, then, let's use this tactic."

I asked for «*Regensburg universität*».

I got a surprisingly long list of universities.

"Look at these, Ralph. Does one of them look familiar?"

I allowed some time for Ralph to peruse down the list as I scrolled slowly down.

"Wait, stop," he ordered, then just as quickly he said, "No, never mind."

"Well," I said. Let's start with the most obvious one. *Institut für Germanistik der Universität Regensburg.*"

I quickly clicked on it, went to the departments, found one called *Didaktik der deutschen Sprache und Literatur,* clicked on it, then found «*Facultät*». Rather nervously I clicked on it, and out popped a list of faculty members with their pictures besides their short bio. I scrolled down, not too far, there weren't too many professors in this department, and—lo, and behold!—we found Dr. Theophilus Ralph all the way at the end, with no picture and out of alphabetical order for there were two teachers before him whose names started with 'S' and 'Z'.

"Gott im Himmel!" cried Ralph within me.

"What is it?" I asked.

"It says here that I'm on leave. Sick leave. It instructs any of my previous students to get in contact with the department chair, in case they need letters of recommendation or to view their final exams."

"Sick leave, huh," I said. "Do you remember having to take sick leave, Ralph? Do you remember getting sick?"

"No, I have no recollection of this. The last thing I remember was that I was teaching my regular classes: I had two Beginners, one Intermediate, and the first Survey of French Lit. In the Beginners' classes we were doing direct and indirect object pronouns; in the Intermediate we were doing *Passé Composé* versus the *Imparfait*; in the literature class we were doing Rabelais versus Marguerite de Navarre. Yes, I had just given out the reading of her *Heptaméron,* which was her version of Boccacio's *Décaméron* but which she was unable to finish since death overtook her suddenly. We were reading the story of the French gentleman Bernage who, while traveling in Germany, seeks hospitality at a château where he observes a sad state of affairs: every day, the lord of the castle makes his adulterous wife drink out of a most remarkable vessel, made of the cranium of her dead lover, two pieces of silver sealing the eye sockets."

"I remember that one," I said. "It's one of my favorites. The husband put the rest of the lover's skeleton in the closet." I chuckled. "That's probably where we got that expression from, 'a skeleton in the closet.' "

After a pause, I asked, "But Ralph, that's all you remember?"

"I'm trying... I'm trying to remember... Everything is so vague, so hazy. It's like watching my past through fog, the fog won't let me get through..."

Ralph's situation saddened me. I felt that something bad had happened to him, since he was no longer with his body.

"Let me write an email to the head of the department. What's his name?"

"Rudolf Schulthess," said Ralph immediately. Some details he hadn't forgotten.

"Yes, Rudolf Schulthess. I'll write him an email, saying that I want to ask you questions about your book on world religions. What do you think?"

Ralph sounded apprehensive. "It sounds like the thing to do, if we want to find out what happened to me."

"All right, then. Shall I write it in English?"

"Yes, go ahead. *Herr* Schulthess knows English very well."

"Super. Here goes: 'I am a professor of French at Florida Southeastern University and wish to contact Professor Ralph who teaches in your department. I looked up Professor Ralph's information on your university's website in order to contact him about his publication *The War of the Gods, from Roncesvalles to New York*, but saw that he is on sick leave. Would you be able to tell me if there is a way for me to contact him? I would like to, like to...' Why do I need to contact you?"

"You're planning a publication on the Religious Right of America and you need my permission to use a quote from my book."

"Hey, that sounds great. 'I would like to ask for his permission to use a quote from his book in a publication of my own about the Religious Right of America.' What do you think?"

"It sounds natural. You'll let me know when his response arrives?"

"Sure, but won't you be here?"

"I don't know. I need to go collect my thoughts. I'm rather afraid."

"I know you are. But don't worry. I'm here with you."

"That you are, my friend, that you are. You are inescapably here with me."

"Hey, I don't mind. Who best to be with, huh? I think you were sent to me because I was ready to receive you. I wasn't the type to go off the deep end, I didn't go crying to a therapist, I didn't go screaming to a priest to have you exorcised, and I didn't start taking pills to abort you."

"Thank you for that, my friend. If ever I can be of any support to you, you let me know."

"You'll be the first person I ask, be sure of that."

Ralph went away, to wherever he goes when he's not with me, and I remained by myself, alert to any answer coming back from the University of Regensburg.

Ralph came back a couple of days later, before any answer had arrived, wishing to find out more about my novel, *The Many Lives of Webster Buchanan*.

"Wow," I said. "What is it about? Well, it's about a supposedly straight guy who lives a very straight life. I made him a financial investor who is straight as an arrow, that is, honest, who would never swindle his clients, who takes his work seriously. He wants to make sure that his client, the little old lady, has enough money to last out her life, that his client, the paterfamilias, has a fortune to leave to his children, etc. But as soon as the sun sets, he becomes gay, ardently, ravenously gay.

He lives alone, and after a couple of cocktails he goes out. He's abandoned his straight-laced coat and tie for cool threads, he leaves his stodgy Mercedes in the garage to get into his Alfa Romeo Spider. He spends the night all the way to dawn patrolling the streets, searching for other gays, cruising in the bars and clubs, fraternizing with young men, spending the night looking for love. But he must be home by dawn. At dawn, he takes his shower and dresses and goes out into the world again dressed as a meek, unadventurous financial investor."

"When does he sleep?"

"He doesn't need to sleep. He's like a superhuman that way. Or, rather, the investor goes to sleep as the gay playboy goes out."

"I thought you were a well-adjusted gay man."

"What do you mean? Of course, I am. Ever since college."

"But your story makes out the gay as being the dark, immoral man to the investor's good and virtuous man."

"Where did you get the idea that it's a tale of good versus evil?"

"Well, the day and night, light and dark, diurnal for the investor, nocturnal for the gay playboy. Yin and yang."

"Well, the clubs only open at night."

"But you made your investor morally straight; so the other side must be sinister and unscrupulous. Usually, promiscuity is viewed as being on the sleazy side."

"Well, that's just it! I wanted to explore the other side of the coin. Just because I go to bed with more people than someone else does not make me sleazy. Unchaste, yes, but not depraved. Promiscuous gays are not depraved. They're just looking for love like the rest of us, only more avidly."

"If you say so. But you're going to have to give your investor some bad qualities. He's a goody two-shoes, and why isn't *he* looking for love? And your gay playboy is too dark, too vampire-like. He waits for the dark, then he comes out fangs first."

"Well, it's a work in progress."

"Don't get defensive. I'm just an expert of literature giving you a little feedback. Your story has great merit, but you can't assign such absolutes to your characters. Otherwise it becomes an allegory."

"Well, I've always loved allegories. *Le Roman de la Rose* is wonderful! You have all of these figures protecting the Rose in the garden, the ideal garden which sounds like Eden to me, then comes Danger and, and… I forget what else, to threaten the Virtue of the Rose. There's real conflict there. You fear for the Rose."

"I could never ever the virtues of virginity accept! It's ludicrous in today's world. It's passé, outmoded. Why men wanted their women untouched and unused is a mystery to me. To say nothing of the double standard. Gallant men have experience and knowledge. Pretty little virtuous damsels cannot have anything placed between their legs or between their ears. Empty, empty, like gourds used for birds' nests."

"Let's not get into that. Women have no place in my novel. I decided from the beginning that there would be no women in my novel."

"What about the little old lady who's a client of the investor?"

"That was just an example. It's not even in the novel. But if I do place it in the novel, I'll make sure to change it to a little old man, a widower, with no daughters."

"It's your novel. You can do with it whatever you want."

"Thank you, thank you, Dr. Ralph, for your permission to do with my novel whatever I want."

"I didn't mean to irritate you. I was just giving advice."

"Yes, yes, I understand. I need to make my investor a little bit wicked, and my playboy a little less depraved. Got it. Let's move on."

"Okay," said Ralph. "I've got something to attend to. See you soon."

Then I was alone. I felt sad that I had chased him away, but I do get touchy sometimes when people criticize my writing and it is obvious that they have no idea as to what I'm doing. My writing has layers and layers of stuff. It's not readily available to most readers. I write for the intelligent reader, who knows his history and the history of literature. The allusions and references to other works is everywhere in my writing. I expect the reader to catch the intertextualities, like readers catch the symbolism in poetry, and realize why they are there in my text. Remember, text and textile are etymological cousins. A writer weaves his text with the warp of human endeavor and the woof of literature. I usurp this material to use in my text. This is all I have, this understanding that I get from the past. It is an imperfect association with generation after generation of people who have been through this existence and thought about our place in the universe and have left their traces in their writing. After all is said and done, after we have lived our lives of quiet desperation or loud belligerence and our generation is put to sleep, all we have ever had is the conversation we had with each other, the connections we had with the past, and the shreds of meaning we hope to leave to the future.

When an email finally arrived in my inbox, Ralph was nowhere near me. There was no way to reach him. This time I tried again, mightily, straining my mind to reach out to him. I even tried yelling in my mind, the way you sometimes dream that you are yelling during a nightmare. All I got in return was silence, deep reverberating silence.

I should have waited for him so that together we could read the message, but I was way too curious and impatient. I looked down at the body of the email and read:

I am very sorry for the delay of this response, but Professor Schulthess is on administrative leave and won't be back until the beginning of next term. I am serving as acting head of the Department of Foreign Languages until he returns.

It is with a sad heart that I must inform you that *Herr* Dr. Ralph is not available. He suffered a stroke last term and is in hospital in a coma. He is a dear colleague of ours, has been with us for decades, and his absence is painful to us all. We pray that he will eventually make a full recovery and that he can once again be among us and among his students who love him. He is a special man, a Mensch, a professor of high caliber and great intellectuality, a Mentor to our younger faculty. We miss him terribly.

In the meantime, I recommend that you get in touch with the publisher in order to get the permission you need for your publication. I don't foresee any complications in that regard. *Herr* Professor's book, *The War of the Gods, from Roncesvalles to New York,* has been very popular and influential in both fields of history and theology.

Thank you very much for your kind interest.

Please don't hesitate to contact me if you have any further questions,

Paul Müller-Schmidt
Interim Department Chairperson
Institute of German Languages and Literature
University of Regensburg

My stomach lurched at this news. *Herr* Dr. Ralph was alive, but he had suffered a stroke and was now in a coma. Damn! His mind was not with his body. He was here with me, far from Regensburg, halfway around the world in Miami, Florida!

What was this? Astral projection? Out of body teleportation? Here was proof that the mind can leave the body! His body was in the hospital. His mind was here, with me. He came here for safekeeping! Whatever state of affairs brought him to me knew that I would keep him secure, protected. All of a sudden, I felt great, that something out there knew that I would be worthy of keeping another anima out of harm's way. I felt positive. Any entity that would have delivered Ralph to me must be thinking that this is temporary, and that when the physical *Herr* Dr. Ralph improves, then he'll need his consciousness back. Something went wrong with his body, with his brain, and it was convalescing. All we had to do was wait until he got better. Then he'd be taken back, and his mind would be in his brain once again.

I could hardly wait to tell Ralph all about this. He would be shocked by the terrible news I got from Regensburg, but he would surely agree with my conjecture that all of this was temporary.

Ralph didn't return for a few days and when he did he asked me for a favor. I said yes, of course, with no hesitation whatsoever. Up to now his favors had been easy, except for the trip to Regensburg, which I was now assuming would be necessary, sooner rather than later.

But this favor threw me for a loop. He asked me if he could be present the next time I was making love to Bo.

"Ralph, I don't think that's a good idea."

"It'll be okay. Why don't you think it's a good idea?"

"Well, for one, you're not gay. You might be disturbed by some of the things... you know... you know?"

"Ah, Rick, I don't care, I really don't care. I've been feeling so lonely in here. Not alone, mind you, because I know I have you. But I'm feeling lonely. I miss people. I miss love. I miss the contact of another human. I need warmth and affection. The only things I can embrace here are the dark and the cold, and my arms ache for the presence of another. I promise I won't mind that it's with another guy. I just want to hug someone. To feel someone hugging me back."

I began to cry. Big fat tears rolling down my cheeks. That a soul was suffering to such an extent under my supervision was unendurable. I felt now what it must be like to have your child suffer while you cannot alleviate her pain.

"Yes, Ralph," I said between sniffles. "Of course you can be with us. Bo won't mind, I mean, he won't know. I'll keep things to a minimum, you know, we'll just cuddle and kiss. It'll be fine, I know."

"Thank you, Rick. I appreciate this so much."

"Okay. It's okay. But for the moment, I need to tell you something."

"You received an answer from Regensburg."

"That's right. Three days ago. There's no way to sugar-coat this, so let me just tell it to you directly. Are you sitting down?"

"I don't know. Why don't you just sit down?"

"Okay, I'll sit down. The head of your department at the university is on leave, so somebody else is serving as interim chair. He informed me that *Herr* Dr. Ralph, that you... that you had a stroke last term and that you are now in the hospital in a coma."

Silence greeted me.

"Ralph? Ralph, are you there?"

"I'm here," he said, with heavy inflection. "I'm here. I suspected something of that nature. Something told me that my brain was not okay, and that I had to leave it. Like a fire going through your house and you have to vacate it while it's being fixed. I hope I'm being fixed. They must be taking care of me at the hospital in Regensburg."

"I'm sure they are, Ralph. "I'm sure they're taking very good care of you."

I dreamt that I was asleep and somebody was talking to me. I couldn't understand the words and it didn't even seem like a language I knew. It wasn't conversation, however, it was just a voice droning on and on about something, like one of my books on tapes. There wasn't much inflection or modulation in the voice, like that of one of the bad narrators that you get sometimes. It felt like hours, and I wanted desperately to wake up and speak with the person belonging to the voice. But I couldn't wake. I couldn't even lift my eyebrows or move my finger. It was as if I were already dead in a casket, but I was still breathing and my heart was still beating. How could I tell this person that I was still alive?

I woke up sweating and panting. Dr. Ralph, unusually, was there.

"Bad dream?" he asked me. "Your heart is racing a mile a minute."

"I had a nightmare," I explained, turning on the lamp beside my bed. Bo was there beside me. I had forgotten he was spending the night. He was still fast asleep. I turned the light off.

I was hot so I pulled down the sheets. I needed to get out of bed. I went into the bathroom in front of the sink and saw my image in the mirror: I looked haggard and my hair was wild. I threw cold water on my face. As I dried myself with a towel I heard Ralph say, "You're pretty shaken up."

"Yes. I dreamt I was dead, or maybe so deeply asleep that I couldn't wake up. But I could hear that somebody was speaking in a low droning voice, as if they were reading to me, maybe reading the last rites."

"What was the person saying?"

"I couldn't understand. It was in a language I don't know."

"Could it have been German?"

"I don't know. I know what German sounds like, but if this was German, it sounded weird, without inflection in the voice, even without intonation patterns. I know the intonation patterns of German, Ralph. It wasn't that."

"Could it have been German spoken by a person with a French accent? French has no intonation patterns to speak of."

"You're right. It is pretty unstressed, not much modulation, as it was in my dream. Her syllables lacked emphasis of any kind, that's for sure."

"It was a female voice?"

"Yes, it was. It was a nice mezzo-soprano voice."

"Rick, I think it was my wife whom you heard. She's French, you know, and she speaks German as if it were French."

"How could I be hearing your wife? I've never even heard her voice. How could I imagine her voice? Wait, are you suggesting that the voice I heard was actually your wife's? Like in real time? It's already morning in Germany. But, come on. Is that even possible? How can you think that?"

"Rick, I was brought here to you. You think anything is impossible now? Do you remember anything she said?"

"Oh, no, nothing. I couldn't even understand it. It was one big long gibberish to me. But wait, I do recognize a name she mentioned, several times. It was 'Roxane.' 'Roxane,' she said. 'Roxane' was in her narration."

"Why do you say narration?"

"Because it sounded like she was reading. The speech was always at the same pitch, no emotion at all, just a recitation."

"Rick, I think it was my wife reading to me."

"If it was your wife reading to you as you lay in bed in a coma, well, then, you should have heard it. Why did I hear it?"

"I don't know, I don't know. But my wife has a low pitch, and she speaks German with no inflection at all, as if she were speaking French. If she were speaking at length, she was probably reading. It would make sense that she would be reading to her comatose husband who is a professor used to reading all the time. She probably wants me to continue reading, or rather, my brain to keep thinking."

"What is your wife's name?"

"Edmée."

I gasped. "Yes, she said it was Edmée. She did announce herself, saying she was Edmée! And she called you *'mon trésor!'* "

This information threw us into a non-verbal moment of disquiet. Neither one of us could say anything. But all at once the lights in the bathroom turned on and I jumped out of my skin.

It was Bo. "Aren't you coming back to bed?" he asked.

"Yes, I was just going back."

"Were you just sick?"

"No, I wasn't. What makes you say that?"

"I heard you making strange gagging noises."

"Oh, I'm sorry. I didn't mean to wake you."

"I need to pee anyway."

Bo did what he came to do and I quickly preceded him back to bed. As I did, I told Ralph that we would continue this conversation in the morning.

Ralph said, "My Edmée was reading to me, Rick. She was reading to me!"

In spite of the excitement, I willed myself to get back in bed. Bo came back from the bathroom and fell into bed next to me, wrapping his body around mine. I wondered if this is what Ralph would have wanted to witness, but I quickly realized that Ralph had gone away to wherever it was that he sequestered himself. It was just as well because Bo fell asleep immediately. All I had time for was to hug him back and kiss him a couple of times. We were in such close contact that we started to sweat on the patches of skin that were touching.

For the rest of the night I didn't dream of any voices reading or not reading.

The next morning, Ralph wanted to find out the name of the hospital where he was staying.

"That's going to be harder than finding out in what university you were teaching," I told him. "But we'll try."

After about a dozen attempts, we could not find a hospital in the city of Regensburg or in its outskirts who had a patient by the name of Theophilus Ralph.

"Maybe the professor at the university can tell us which is the hospital," suggested Ralph.

"But what possible reason could I give for going back to him to ask that? I mean, I'm supposed to direct my attention to the publishers of your book."

"Maybe they will know. Surely the editors will know. The editors always know the whereabouts of their authors."

"I really don't think that's the case in your situation. You're on a different continent now."

"I'm talking about my body. My body is still in Germany. But wait… Wait a minute. Perhaps my body is not in Germany. Maybe I wasn't in Germany when I had my stroke. Maybe I was in France. Edmée and I go to France all the time. Perhaps we went there for Easter break. We always go visit her folks for Easter break."

"Anything is possible. Where does Edmée's family live?"

"They live in Paris."

"Oh, great! There must be hundreds of hospitals in Paris and its suburbs. We'll never find you there!"

"But for Easter they go to their country house, which is located in Nonant, a tiny village in Calvados, in Normandy."[2]

"Never heard of it. Where is that?"

"It's in Normandy. You've heard of Bayeux?"

"Where the tapestry is?"

"Yes. Nonant is a quarter-hour away by car, to the southeast, on the way to Caen."

"Well, is there a hospital nearby?"

---

[2] Calvados is the department where the liqueur *calvados* is made. It has digestive properties which, because of its strength, when taken after a heavy meal supposedly "burns a hole" through the food, allowing the eater to continue to nosh away. Normandy is the origin of the invader William the Conqueror who successfully took over England at the Battle of Hastings in the year 1066, which is the subject of the tapestry of Bayeux. Normandy is also the scene of the Allied invasion that came to rout the Germans in World War II.

"There has to be. Nonant is tiny, but there must be a hospital in Bayeux."

Calling the Bayeux hospitals was easier; there were only two, and I could speak in French. We hit pay dirt with our second call, and we were asked, or rather, I was asked, if I wanted to ring the room. I stammered yes before I realized that somebody might answer, and then I might have to speak to that somebody.

Before I could even think of hanging up, the voice was on the phone. It was unmistakable. I recognized it as the voice that had been droning on and on, perhaps reading to the comatose Ralph.

"Ah, yes," I said in French, "Is this *madame* Ralph?"

"Yes, who is on the phone?"

"It's my wife! It's my wife!" Ralph was yelling in my ear.

"Shush! Stop it, Ralph. You're not letting me listen. I need to speak to your wife!"

"Who is on the phone?" repeated *madame* Ralph.

"I'm… I'm sorry to bother you like this, but… I'm one of the nurses who's been taking care of your husband, and I wanted to ask you what you were reading to your husband… A book… A book…"

"What, this morning?"

"Perhaps, I mean… Yes, yes, this morning. It was quite lovely, and I wish to… I wish to buy it… to read it, I mean…"

"It was *Cyrano de Bergerac*, by Edmond Rostand, but translated into German. It's my husband's favorite play. You understand German?"

"No, I don't… but it was still lovely the way you were reading it… I… I shall read it in French, of course. I haven't read it in years, but I remember it was always a favorite play of mine… I… I… *euh*… How is *monsieur* Ralph?"

There was a pause on the other side before *madame* Ralph

answered, "There has been no change. But he continues to moan, and sigh, which continues to give me hope. Sighs may be insensate actions, but I do not believe they are involuntary. They are attached to how we are feeling. The doctors just say that moaning and groaning could be a manifestation of eructations stemming from his digestive system, but I don't believe it. A sigh is not the same as flatulence, you know? You're a nurse, so you understand very well that doctors think they know everything, but we know they don't, *n'est-ce pas?*"

I didn't know what else to say, so I stammered an agreement, "Yes, I know doctors well, as a matter of fact, I live with one, and I know they're not always right, although they think they are. And they never ever admit to making a mistake!"

"Oh, is it one of the doctors from this hospital?"

"Oh, no, it's a doctor from a faraway hospital. He's... She's..."

What was I saying and doing? I hadn't meant to get myself involved. I turned, inwardly, to Ralph and asked him, "What do I do now?" I was at a complete loss.

"Hello, are you there?" I heard from the phone.

Ralph spoke to me at the same time. He was weeping. "I hear the voice of my wife, Rick. She's there! I need to speak to her!"

A second later I said into the phone, "Yes, yes, I'm still here. Please hold on a second, while I... while I..."

"You can't speak to her!" I told Ralph with as much command as I could muster. "How would you do it? Through me? She won't believe it! She'll think I'm a prankster! I can't... We can't do this to her..."

"Tell her..." said Ralph. "Yes, we can do this! Tell her the following... Stop that! Shut up! You're getting hysterical! Calm down, we can do this. Tell her... Shut up and listen to me! Tell her the following, please tell her the following: '*Madame* Ralph, I have something of importance to tell you.'"

I took the phone firmly in my hand and said, "*Madame* Ralph, I have something of importance to tell you."

"Yes, what is it?" came the response.

Ralph told me what to say next, and I spoke the words into the phone. This was so much easier for me. The control and responsibility had been wrested away from me.

"*Madame* Ralph, there are strange things that happen on Earth that are sometimes… strange, that are… weird, that have no rational explanation… and that every once in a while we have the opportunity to be a witness to something unexplainable… that sometimes is best described as a miracle."

"Yes," came the reaction from the other side, a bit drawn out with nascent vigilance and a healthy dollop of Gallic skepticism.

I dutifully recited Ralph's next statement word for word.

"I am going to tell you something that is known only to you and to *monsieur* Ralph."

"Is this a joke, because if it is, I am not amused by it," was the cold reply of *madame* Ralph. "Are you a nurse here?"

"Edmée, this man on the phone is speaking for me. Listen to what he's saying. He's repeating my words to you."

"What is your name? I am going to report you to the police, you hear me? How dare you—"

" *'Ah, que pour ton bonheur je donnerais le mien,*
Quand même tu devrais n'en savoir jamais rien!' "[3]

"Why did you say that? You are horrible! How did you know this?"

"Edmée, it's me! Please recognize me! You know very well that I am in these words!"

---

[3] From *Cyrano de Bergerac*, by Edmond Rostand: "Oh, for your happiness I would give up mine,/Even if you should never know anything about it!"

"How did you know these lines are my husband's favorites?"

"Because it's me, Edmée. I'm not there with you, my body is, but I am not. I was displaced somehow, and my consciousness is in someone else's mind, and it is he who is speaking for me, but it is your Théo who is speaking to you. Edmée, c'est moi!"

"Tell me then, what is your favorite line from *Phèdre?*"

" '*C'est Vénus tout entière à sa proie attachée!*' "[4]

"What is your favorite line from *Le Cid?*"

" '*Réduit au triste choix ou de trahir ma flamme,*
Ou de vivre en infâme,
Des deux côtés mon mal est infini.' "[5]

"What is your favorite play of all?"

"*On ne badine pas avec l'amour.*"

"What is your favorite line from it?"

"It's when Camille turns to Perdican and says, '*O Perdican! ne raillez pas, tout cela est triste à mourir!*' "[6]

Both Ralph and I heard a scream at the end of the line and then the sound of someone falling. The phone went dead. For a moment, neither one of us said, or thought, anything. The two of us were huddled in the middle of my mind, both blind and deaf to the world outside and to each other. There was nothing to say, nothing to do. There was no escape from the horror of not knowing what had happened to Edmée.

---

[4] From *Phèdre*, by Racine: "It is Venus absolute clutching her prey!"

[5] From *Le Cid*, by Corneille: "Reduced to the sad choice of betraying my passion,/Or to live in infamy,/From both sides my pain is infinite."

[6] From *On ne badine pas avec l'amour*, by Alfred de Musset: "Oh, Perdican, don't jest, all of this is so sad I could die!"

Later that day Ralph was berating himself severely for what had happened.

"We never should have called. We should have gone to France ourselves, and been present to tell all of this to Edmée. Do you think she believed us?"

"Yes, I do think she believed us. She had to. You convinced her that it was you. Who else would have known all your favorite lines from those plays? I think she fainted because she believed you. If she hadn't, she would have been angry and upset and told us to go to hell and that she was going to report us to the police."

"Well, I think we need to go to France now."

I nodded my head before I realized Ralph couldn't see me, so I quickly said, "Yes, let's go. Let's go right away."

I was forced to tell Bo about Ralph. I had to. That same night, after the fiasco with Edmée, Ralph was so upset that he didn't let me sleep. Except that I did sleep. All of this is so confusing! I slept, Ralph did not sleep, and he caused me to get up in the middle of the night and start pacing like a crazy restless sleepwalker. Apparently I was also talking in my sleep. In German. Bo got so disconcerted that he didn't know what to do, but he knew enough that he didn't dare wake me up. Always a doctor first, he had the presence of mind of going back to the bedroom to pick up his iPhone, take it to the living room where I was pacing and yammering *auf Deutsch,* and proceeded to film me, and record me. The following day it was all there, on video, and I got goosebumps watching myself pacing back and forth and listening to myself speaking in a language of which I was, and still am, in complete ignorance, except for *Gott im Himmel* and stuff like that that comes from novels and operas. In my somnambulist state my eyes were open but unseeing. I was focused on some faraway horizon, or perhaps looking inwardly into my brain. I have no idea. I didn't remember any of it. Bo was aghast. He didn't know what to do. He finally did nothing, and after about an hour he just followed me back to bed where I simply got back under the covers. Thank *Gott im Himmel* that I didn't walk out the front door!

In the morning, Bo thought of calling a doctor friend of his, a psychologist. I told him it wouldn't be necessary, unless he wanted to make an appointment for himself.

"What do you mean? I'm not the one who was sleepwalking and sleeptalking in German!"

"Well, there is an explanation, but once I tell you it might be useful for you to have a session with a shrink."

"Yeah, right! I'll be the judge of that. Give me the explanation."

I told Bo the story of Ralph, from the inception to the events of the previous day. I told it as calmly, as rationally as I possibly could. Bo remained pretty much impassive during my explanation, although the furrow between his brows deepened at several instances during my speech. At the end of it, Bo remained silent for a long time, long enough for me to get uncomfortable.

"So, what do you think?" I finally said. "You still think I need a shrink? You must believe me. How else could I have been speaking in German?"

"I don't know," said Bo, "I couldn't tell you why. But I prefer to look for a rational explanation here. This sort of thing… just… can't… happen. It is of no matter how much you believe that it's true. It is not possible, it is not credible, it is not feasible. It doesn't exist in the realm of real possibilities."

There was Bo, my scientist, my Cartesian buddy, my intelligent, cerebral, analytical, logical friend. Ordinarily I would be proud of him. But not today. Not with Ralph bopping around in my mind. Although at this particular instance, Ralph was not with me. After such a restless night, he must have been sleeping.

I went over and over the possible ways I had of convincing Bo about the veracity of my predicament. Ralph helped, too, but together we couldn't come up with a way of making Bo accept the truth of what was happening. Scientific folk are just as bad as religious folk, sometimes, in that they can accept nothing but their beliefs: they hold the scientific method so tightly in their embrace, that they cannot fathom phenomena occurring outside the realm of the methodology which gives meaning to their whole world, their whole universe. To them, everything is black and white, sane or insane, and if anybody holds something that differs, they are cast into the side that is insane. To Bo, his friend and lover was now insane. He watched me now with a look that bordered somewhere between pity, shame, and compassion. He wanted to help me. I, on the other hand, wanted to help him to understand me. To accept the reality of this unworldly phenomenon. I wanted him to accompany me—us!—to France. I wanted him to be present for when I confronted the problem head on. Ralph was within me, but in twenty-four hours we would be standing in front of the comatose Dr. Ralph, the body, and wondering how things were going to fix themselves, if ever. Even though I tried not to form the thought, it sometimes escaped my volition and it flashed across my mind, and I knew that Ralph had "seen" it, or whatever sense is used to notice a thought. Ralph was complicating my life to such a degree that I could not help thinking that he was becoming a sort of nuisance now. The thought came to me involuntarily that I was perhaps getting a bit tired of him. I certainly wished to be hospitable. I could imagine the situation reversed and I, Rick Luna, might have been trapped within Ralph's mind. I would have hoped that he would have been understanding and accommodating. But here I was going to miss a week of classes, I who hardly ever was absent. I had an emergency appendectomy once, but, since it was done laparoscopically on a Saturday I was back in class the following Tuesday, having missed only that Monday. For this coming absence, I was going to have to lie to my department chair, telling her that important business had come up in France and I needed to be there immediately. I also needed to find and prepare a substitute for the time I would be gone. In short, it was a nuisance to go through all this rigmarole, without knowing that our trip to France would have any beneficial consequences. To say nothing of my relationship with Bo. I didn't want to leave him behind, and I certainly didn't want to go by myself. Fortunately, he agreed to come with me to France, but I think he did it out of concern for my sanity. He realized that he couldn't change my mind, I was so galvanized. But he was able to exact a promise from me. In order to leave the country I had to promise him that if things did not go well I would see the shrink upon my return. As far as he was concerned, I had an idée fixe that neither he nor I could dislodge, and he feared that my mental health would deteriorate if he had me Baker-acted. Such a move would go on my record, everybody would find out about it, my family, my friends, my colleagues at school, and, in effect, I would be branded a bona-fide loony. Besides, Bo could still not prove that I was a threat either to myself or to anyone else. He was already a few steps ahead of me in that regard: what would the psychiatrist do with me? Perhaps give me medication, perhaps order a stint in some psychiatric ward. They would not be able to hold me for long, and then what would Bo do? I asked Bo to trust me, to just trust me, that I was not going crazy. I even asked him to play along. Even if I were insane, even if my obsession with a supposed supplementary personality were true, he should let me get this trip out of my system. I felt that it could help Ralph, it couldn't hurt him, and it certainly couldn't hurt me. I even tried to induce some enthusiasm about going to France, a place that Bo also loved to visit.

I made reservations for two, even though three of us were traveling.

I barely heard from Ralph during the flight to Paris and hardly anything after we rented a car to go to Bayeux. Tired and disheveled as we were, I knew that Ralph was impatient to get to the hospital and see his wife and… and himself.

We were in Bayeux at the hospital at a quarter to noon. Even though Bo felt super uncomfortable going to see this patient, a complete stranger, he stuck with me. When we were just outside the door I looked at him with gratitude, took a deep breath, asked Ralph if he was ready, and after his affirmative response I walked in, Bo following me. There was no one in the room save for the patient.

"I wonder where *madame* Ralph is?" I said out loud so that Bo could hear me as well.

"It's nearly lunchtime," answered Bo.

"She's gone to have lunch," responded Ralph simultaneously.

We approached the bed.

There was a rotund man there, mostly bald, attached like a fetus to strange apparatuses, only with the tubes coming out of his nose, a transparent plastic mask covering both his nose and mouth. I supposed that the machine was breathing for him. Other than the rhythmic hum of the apparatus, along with regular pinging from other smaller contraptions arrayed behind the bed, there was complete silence. Ralph ordered me to approach the bed.

Bo said, "I don't think we should approach the patient."

"But Ralph wants to see him," I explained.

"You realize nobody else is going to see Ralph, either," said Bo.

"Of course I know this, but Ralph wants to examine his body."

"Oh, my God. We are so going to get into trouble. We're neither friends nor family!"

"No, it's better than that. One of us *is* the patient. And he wants to see himself."

By this time, I was standing right in front of the comatose man. Bo had decided to stay by the door, like a sentinel guarding the only exit.

Ralph instructed me to touch the patient's hand. I did, and we both observed that it felt cool. I went ahead and felt around his wrist for his pulse. It was weak, but regular. We could see his heartbeat delineated in measured patterns on one of the screens as if they were musical notes on a pentagram repeated ad infinitum. I looked over my shoulder and asked Bo if the heart diagram looked okay. Bo took a step closer to observe and responded affirmatively. Seeing other screens and other machines, he walked the rest of the way, as if curious to see a patient who was in trouble, and perhaps willing to offer a clinical interpretative view. Bo was an excellent doctor; his patients loved him. He always wanted to help.

"His heart monitor indicates his heart is strong and regular; his pressure is fine," he announced. "His color's a bit pale; but his fingernails are pink. Everything's been attended to: he's on an automatic sphygmomanometer, he's receiving nutrition through a naso-gastric tube, oxygen through a face mask. There is nothing else to do for a comatose man. There is nothing additional that you and I can do for him."

"Ralph says that he looks like he's sleeping."

Bo took his iPhone out of his pocket and turned on the flashlight. He raised an eyelid of the patient and shone the light directly into his right eye.

"Oh, careful," I said. "It's too bright."

Bo observed for a few seconds, removing the phone and then placing it over Ralph's left eye and repeating the movement a couple of times.

"His pupil is fixed and dilated, with no change whatsoever when I shine the light directly into his eye. He's in a coma alright."

Ralph instructed me to put a palm on the patient's forehead, which I did without hesitation.

"Don't touch him," warned Bo. "Why do you want to invite trouble?"

"I'm not inviting trouble. Ralph wanted to feel his forehead. I don't feel a fever. He's cool to the touch."

"What did you expect?" asked Bo. "He's in a coma. His brain is obviously affected, but the rest of his body is okay."

I pointed to one of the machines. "Not his lungs. He's not breathing on his own."

"Of course, he's breathing on his own. That's not a ventilator. The mask is just to direct oxygen into his lungs, but they are functioning. His respiratory system is functioning, his digestive system, too. The NG tube is to keep his GI tract active, otherwise he'd just have IV fluids going into a vein. It could have been far more serious: his medulla oblongata could have been affected, but apparently it wasn't. Ralph is right, he is asleep, but the prognosis that he'll wake up anytime soon is not good. I'm sure his brain scans show no activity."

I was happy that for the first time Bo had mentioned the name of Ralph as if he were another entity, as opposed to my hallucination.

A voice from the doorway startled us all.

"Who are you?" we heard in French. "What are you doing here?"

We turned around and saw a small, delicate woman holding a bag and a plastic glass in her hands.

"It's Edmée!" shouted Ralph in my ear. In my surprise and enthusiasm I reacted instantaneously and also shouted, "It's Edmée!"

Edmée came into the room, an eyebrow raised and a quizzical expression on her face, but her mouth set as if getting ready to reprimand us.

I immediately explained, "I'm *monsieur* Luna from America, and this is my friend Dr. Solomon who's accompanied me."

Edmée seemed to brighten with this last detail. Putting her things down on a tray by the foot of the bed she asked, "You are a doctor? From the United States?"

I translated for Bo and answered for him, "Yes, he is. He's an endocrinologist. He's affiliated with both Cedars and Jackson Memorial in Miami, which is the city where I'm from as well."

She walked over to us and shook our hands.

"Ever since you spoke to me on the phone I have been thinking and thinking, but I cannot come to the conclusion that you want me to accept. I cannot understand how the mind (*l'esprit,* she said in French) of my husband is no longer with him, that it somehow catapulted thousands of miles away in Miami and you are now… sharing his consciousness along with your own."

"This could have happened when we were in France last. We were in Paris, and then we traveled through Normandy. We came to see the tapestry. I don't know to what extent distance plays as a factor, but we were very close. In any case, he could have been in my mind for weeks, maybe a couple of months. As far as I can understand, *monsieur* Ralph was in my mind for a while before he made his presence known to me. I believe he was asleep for a long time, and then reticent to communicate with me. He wasn't even aware that he could speak to me. It could have been a long while before I knew he was here with me."

I held up a finger to ask for a moment while Ralph said something to me. He wanted me to hug her. I told him I could not, that I should not, since I was just meeting her. But he insisted, so I told Edmée what he wanted.

"*Monsieur* Ralph wants to hug you," I said.

Edmée burst into tears. She put a hand to hide her face and turned halfway around. "I can't," she said. "I can't. I still don't believe… I cannot believe…"

I translated to Bo what was going on, and he offered a statement, which I translated to her, "*Madame* Ralph, I still don't believe it, either. But we're here now. Let's get to the bottom of this. I've never known my friend to be delusional or obsessional, but we've crossed the Atlantic in the hope, in the dire hope, of being able to help your husband. How could Rick have possibly known all the way in Miami that your husband was in trouble here in France? Is there an explanation for such a mystery? We need to get to the bottom of this."

That phrase, 'We need to get to the bottom of this,' which Bo repeated, was difficult to translate into French. The first time I translated it as, *"Il faut approfondir tout ceci,"* which is closer to "We need to inquire into all of this." The second time I translated it as, *"Il faut que nous atteignions le but de tout ceci,"* which is closer to "It is necessary for us to reach our objective with this."

Edmée's eyes were red and she looked distraught. Clenching one of her hands in the other she said, "The doctors want to detach Théo from all the machines. They say there is no hope. There is no brain function. He will never regain consciousness. The coma is permanent."

Again she burst into tears.

I translated for Bo what she had said and he asked her if the doctors had generated a prognosis based on the Glasgow Coma Scale. I translated without understanding what that was, but Edmée knew right away. She responded that the doctors thought the coma was deep-seated, persistent and had affected even some involuntary movements like swallowing. There were no brain functions whatsoever.

Bo's expression was grave. Edmée had tears flowing down her cheeks. I addressed her with as much compassion as I could muster. "I, on the contrary, think there *is* hope. I am proof of that. It was he (and I pointed to the body lying before us) who called me here. *Monsieur* Ralph is alive and conscious and within me! He can speak with you. He can speak with you through me, like you have been speaking with Bo, with me translating. But I believe we can try for him to speak to you directly. Two nights ago he had me sleepwalking and speaking in German, so obviously he had taken over the functioning of my body while I was asleep. I can try to fall asleep now, and maybe he'll come out and be able to speak to you directly, without my intervention."

Ralph was ecstatic inside me. He was doing mental cartwheels and shouting in glee. "Yes, yes, yes, let's try it. It could work, yes it could!"

I said, "I'm so tired after the flight anyway, I don't think it will be hard for me to fall asleep."

After Bo found out what *monsieur* and *madame* Ralph and I had decided, I sat down on the only chair in the room and proceeded to get comfortable. I looked around me rather nervously, for I had three people staring at me, two standing in front of me and one crouching within me, who were waiting for me to fall asleep. My mind was careering all over the place, but my body was tired. I concentrated on the fatigue in my body, in my feet, first of all, then in my legs. I proceeded to be as conscious as possible of the fatigue in my body as I went up it in my mind, doing the inventory of the fatigue of my corporeal self. By the time I got up to my shoulders and neck, I had done a pretty good job of self-hypnosis for I have no recollection of what happened next.

Did I dream? Did I imagine? Did I fantasize? Did I create illusions, a fiction of chimaeras and figments of feigned reality? Was it tantamount to immersing myself in the world of generating fiction, a world I loved because it allowed me an infinity of creativity, of inspiration, free to innovate effusive tales of mirages and reflections that *did not exist,* of phantasmagoria that appeared and developed full-blown out of thin air but in the end only represented counterfeit imitations of the real? They felt real to me, but I was away, in a different world, floating on soothing waves which by their soporific regularity kept me somnolent and hypnotized. I felt images, sounds, vibrations through my body, but I felt them as though through the drunkenness of sleep, of temporarily being unconscious.

Ralph, however, Ralph the patient, the body with the sick brain, was forever unconscious. Next to his motionless body, his mind, unbeknownst to me, sprang forth to replace me and take control of my body. It was he who manipulated my limbs, moved my lips and tongue to speak, who looked through my eyes and saw his pretty, diminutive wife whom he obviously adored. I, or rather he, took her hands into his and brought them up to his lips to kiss them and weep over them.

By this time, Bo, my precious scientist, my loving and intelligent partner, had readied his iPhone to commit the images and sounds to posterity, and that is the only way I had of knowing what I did, or rather, of what *monsieur* Ralph did.

"Edmée," he began. For some reason he chose French to speak with his wife. "Edmée, you must try to see my spirit through the eyes of this benevolent person. Neither he nor I had control over what happened. Whatever mechanism made my consciousness jump from my mind to somebody else's, it also chose the person who received me. We had never met before, and as you can see, we are very different, physically. The only thing we have in common is that we are both teachers of French."

"And he is also very sensitive," ventured Edmée.

"Indeed he is, and very generous. He has not asked for a single sou for rent."

Edmée laughed.

"Ah, that's the Edmée I know. You should no longer weep. I am here, with you. I need to convince you of this. Edmée, your father died of alcohol poisoning. Everybody else thinks he died of a heart attack. Our first kiss was under a linden tree in the Bois the Boulogne after we had gone to visit the Rose Garden. We were interrupted by a transvestite who called us nincompoops for being in her territory. Your dissertation director was in love with you, and you knew it, but you wanted to finish fast, get your diploma and get the hell out of Chicoutimi. Your favorite wine is from Pauillac; your favorite chocolate is from la Marquise de Sévigné; your favorite restaurant is Le Ruc; your favorite museum is the Rodin; your favorite perfume is L'Air du Temps; your favorite meal is bœuf bourguignon with pasta. Our last argument was because I received a gift from a student, a decorative plate from Verona depicting Romeo looking up at Juliet in her garden, and you told me I should give it back. I told you it wasn't necessary; the student was a good student, not fishing for good grades, and furthermore had no feelings for me. You were jealous, *petite* Edmée, you were jealous of a student whose name I don't even remember now."

"Paola was her name!" cried out Edmée. "It was Paola, and she did have feelings for you. You just didn't realize it!"

With that, Edmée flung herself into the arms of her husband's host, or landlord, or symbiont, namely me. It was difficult afterwards to see me hugging and kissing Edmée on her cheeks and eyes and forehead. Bo was holding the phone, which was shaking a bit, so I couldn't see his expression, but what must have gone through his thoughts as he witnessed this scene!

The moment didn't last long, for there was a sudden irruption into the room. Four doctors, three men and a woman, walked in, one of them holding a pile of papers in his hand.

It was the disconnect clique, there to detach the hapless Ralph from all his tubes. With legal papers from the hospital's attorneys, they swarmed all over the apparatuses and started to detach all tubes, wires, masks, cannulae, and catheters. They unplugged everything from the wall sockets. All Edmée, Ralph and Bo could do was stand and watch them put asunder everything that was helping Ralph's body to stay alive. By the time they left, Ralph was completely unplugged. Not even his heart monitor was left on. No oxygen, either. The patient was liberated to follow whatever destiny was before him, even if that were simply to die.

After the commotion and noise of the four physicians was over, the room was left to the silence and vigilance of its original four occupants, one of whom remained in a coma, and another, deeply asleep, in complete ignorance of what had just transpired.

Veux-tu me compléter et que je te complète?
Tu marcheras, j'irai dans l'ombre à ton côté:
Je serai ton esprit, tu seras ma beauté.

[Do you want to complete me and me to complete you?
As you walk, I'll follow in the shadow beside you:
I will be your mind, you will be my beauty.][7]

This is how Ralph explained our symbiosis to Edmée. This German French teacher who had had a stroke and had to vacate his head, became the "other person inside my head." He lacked a physical place of residence and had taken up lodgings with me. Neither one of us was really each other's beauty, and we both had spirit, mind, wits, brains enough for one person to reconnoiter through life, but the metaphor provided by Rostand was apt. I was propping Ralph up, making space for him, we hoped temporarily, until that time when he could go "back home." When this time was, neither one of us knew. But we certainly were expecting some kind of event if Ralph's body died. Now that he wasn't receiving any medical support from the hospital, this was only a matter of time. Ralph's body could not get sustenance and he would starve to death. For the moment, he was breathing on his own, but we were afraid that it would cease as well.

---

[7] Edmond Rostand, *Cyrano de Bergerac*, Act II, scene 10.

If his body died and Ralph's consciousness, not being able to go back into his head, remained with me forever, well, I suppose I would find that it would impinge on my own existence. It would be like having a foreign, although rather pleasant, person living with you in your bedroom all the time. How much of a bother would it be, I couldn't tell, for I tried not to formulate the thought, but Ralph caught a whiff of it anyway and tried to console me with the probability that his consciousness would vanish at the same time of his body's physical death. I responded that I would not like that at all, that, in effect, having been companions for this time, bosom buddies as it were, I felt a responsibility for him and would mind terribly if both his body and mind passed away.

"Ralph, you can stay with me for as long as you like," I told him. I meant it, too.

"But I don't know how I can live without Edmée who truly is my better half!"

"Ralph, don't cry. Please don't cry."

As mysterious as this whole thing had been up to now, and a complete surprise to the two of us, I was hoping for another miracle, another hell of a surprise! I told him as much.

"But we don't believe in miracles, you and I. We're Eighteenth-century humanists and atheists. We don't believe in denouements that arrive with thunder accompanying a grotesque deus ex machina who descends from the rafters to clear everything up, punish the guilty, reward the good, and at the end of it all, everybody gets to go home. Sometimes, in real life, some people don't get to go home."

I allowed Ralph to borrow my body a few times while Bo and I remained in France. I suppose that Ralph didn't misuse it since it was serving as his body, too. I trusted him implicitly not to pour alcohol into it, save for maybe a kir as an apéritif and a couple of glasses of red wine with dinner. He was no smoker so I was sure that he wouldn't pollute my lungs with carcinogenic smoke. But we were, after all, in Normandy, so a postprandial snifter of Calvados would have been in the offing. I would not deny him that. Each time he made use of my body it was for only a few hours at a stretch, save for the last time. It was at night, I needed to get a good night's rest for the flight the following day, and we didn't know when Ralph was going to see Edmée next. We were all staying in Edmée's family's country home in the rural area outside Caen, a part of Normandy I've always liked for its rolling hills and beautiful apple and pear orchards. Each time Ralph borrowed my body, I was, of course, asleep, so I was not aware of how he was using me. I assumed they went for a walk, went out to dinner, sat in the beautiful garden at dawn overlooking a field of sunflowers. Ralph's own body had been placed in one of the upstairs bedrooms where it was warmer, and we all took turns going up to look in on him and turn him over to avoid bed sores. His body looked so pitiable, so small and alone. In just the week we were there Bo and I could tell that he had lost weight, even though he was managing to swallow energy drinks and liquid vitamins.

In the morning of our departure, Edmée thanked me for the opportunities to allow her to speak to her husband directly.

She informed me that Théo felt like an interloper for taking over my body, even though it was with my permission. I told her that it was my pleasure; I wouldn't want to remain incommunicado with Bo for any length of time, either. If it had been the other way around, I'm sure that Ralph would have granted me permission to have moments of privacy with Bo. I was glad to be of help, I told her. Then Edmée said something which at first I didn't understand. She said that Ralph felt a bit like a cuckoo.

I answered, "Just because this weird thing has happened doesn't make him crazy."

Edmée smiled. "No, he means a real cuckoo, the bird. You know how cuckoos have the habit of laying their eggs in the nests of other, smaller birds. When the baby cuckoo hatches, days before the host bird's eggs, the baby cuckoo pushes his unhatched step-siblings out of the nest until only it remains. The host parents keep feeding it until it's grotesquely huge, much bigger than themselves, but they never realize they've been fooled. That's why he feels like a cuckoo, because every time he takes over your body he feels a little bit guilty."

"But in this case it is with my permission. And I'm sure he's not scheming to 'push me out of the nest.' I don't think that that is possible, anyway. Eventually I wake up, and as soon as I wake up I regain my own consciousness, my own awareness, my own memories. Of course I have no memories of the time that he is in control of my body. So long as he doesn't misuse or abuse my body, it's okay with me if he takes over for a while. I need to sleep, anyway. So he might as well put my body to good use."

Edmée looked a bit weird when I talked about misusing my body, but the whole situation was so beyond weird that I didn't think anything of it. It was time to go back home, and I was a bit nervous about how the absence of her husband's conscience was going to affect Edmée. I knew they had lots to say to each other, but when I went home, Ralph was going to have to hitch the ride with me. We were like conjoined twins, only conjoined internally. We were kindred spirits as well, joined spiritually. Biologically, we were symbionts, cooperating with each other. In the end, perhaps, we were a little bit like Cyrano and Christian, not that we were both in love with the same woman, but in that we complemented each other, or perhaps augmented each other. We were greater than our separate parts. We were a good team, a great duo. It was a very sad day for all of us when we had to say goodbye to Edmée. She was inconsolable.

When Bo confirmed our flights for the return home, he almost wrote Ralph's name down as well. I was happy to know that Bo was now fully a convert and believed without a doubt that I was harboring another person inside my psyche. This was truly an admirable feat for a doctor. I know that Edmée was convinced, perhaps even more so, if one may speak of degrees of belief. I mean, how can one say 'I believe a little bit in God'? Either one believes in something invisible or not. I know that Edmée believed that her husband was living inside my head, as it was corroborated a little bit later. As we left Nonant for the train station that would take us to Caen and then on to Paris, little did we know that we were leaving Edmée pregnant with her husband's child. Only it wasn't Ralph's child; it was more like mine, since the sole anatomy available during the proceedings could only have belonged to me. None of us believed in a second immaculate conception.

So, who was the cuckoo in this situation, me? Or my symbiont interloper?

PART 2

The semester was going strong and because of my excursion to France I had lost a full week of classes. I had sort of lied to my chairperson, Dr. López, telling her that I was attending a very important Eighteenth-century literary convocation. I told myself that since Dr. Ralph and I were both *dix-huitiémistes,* anytime we met we were having a "convocation" of sorts. I was a living, breathing, movable "convocation" then, ever collaborating, ever consorting, ever exchanging ideas with my fellow homologue. We were an inseparable committee, one with instantaneous communication, and constant and intimate association.

However, coming back, even after just a week's absence, was difficult. Even though I had left good professors to substitute for me, there's nothing like teaching the lessons yourself. I found one class very confused about pronouns, so I had to take two sessions just to review the direct object pronouns, the indirect object pronouns, and *"y"* and *"en."* Most students would prefer never to use pronouns at all, but I tell them that language without pronouns sounds stilted and unnatural. I have a pretty good methodology to teach students the difference between transtitive and intransitive verbs, and Ralph came up with excellent exercises, so between the two of us working in tandem we did a great job. Final exams weren't far away, and we had a lot of ground to cover. It was great having the extra help. I felt guilty that Ralph wasn't drawing a salary.

When the German professor in my department, *Fräulein* Doppelgänger, got the flu a few weeks later, it was Ralph's idea for me, that is, for us, to offer our services as a substitute for her. In my office right before one of her classes I self-hypnotized and my German homologue took over. His teaching activities didn't even tire me. On the contrary, I took several naps those few days, while he taught German. One of the students in

Beginning German, who was also in my French lit class, came during my office hours to tell me that my personality changed when I spoke in German. I told her that I already knew that I was more outgoing and social when I was in France speaking French. I was more introverted and taciturn whenever I was in Spain speaking Spanish. I asked her for her opinion about my "German" personality. She said that I was much more patient and kind.

"I am cruel and heartless in French class?"

"No, of course you're not, but you are more cynical, more… brooding, like, more complicated; less compassionate."

"I would have thought that the German language would have made me more rigorous and demanding," I responded.

This made Ralph bolt upright within me. He said, "There you go again, attributing who knows what stereotypes to a whole language and culture."

"If the Teutonic shoe fits, then wear it," I said, none too genially.

The student thought I was speaking to her, so I quickly added, "But then again, the Germans have Schiller, and Goethe, who were very sweet, not so grandiosely austere."

She looked at me unblinkingly, as if attempting to surmise my comedic sincerity.

I turned jocular, to appease her, and cried out, "I must be tapping into the German Romantics when I teach German. When I teach French I must be tapping into the Existentialists!"

She laughed and I felt relieved. I shouldn't let myself be goaded by Ralph into speaking out loud when other people are present. It could get me into trouble.

I t did get me into trouble with the law.

In our county it is against the law to drive while speaking on a cell phone. One day I was driving and, for some unknown reason, I was vocalizing while speaking with Ralph. Most of the time I would just think my responses to my internal interlocutor, but when we were all alone and there was no danger of anybody else listening to what I had to say, I would speak out loud. Well, a cop must have thought I was on the cell phone because he stopped me on my way back home one afternoon. We were on Dixie Highway with its killer traffic, so it took me some time to duck into a strip mall, with the cop hot on my tail, where we wouldn't block anybody.

I asked Ralph, "Did you see me do something wrong? Was I speeding?"

"No, nothing," was Ralph's answer.

The cop, however, had a different version. "You were on the phone," he chided as he began to write me a citation. "Driver's license and registration, please."

"I was not on the phone," I told him. This was the truth.

"For the past five miles, since we got off I-95, you've been yammering away." The cop offered this as incontrovertible fact. "Driver's license and registration, please," he repeated.

"I may have been yammering away, but I was not on the phone. All you have to do is look at my phone and see for yourself. You will see that there are no recent calls, either outgoing, or incoming." I offered him my phone to inspect.

"You've emptied it. It's not difficult to do. You erased all recent information."

"You can do that? I don't know how to do that."

I thought my technological ignorance would get me a grain of sympathy. But either people lacking in sympathy are attracted to become cops, or else the training to become cops forever erased all human empathy from them.

"This is the last time I'll ask you nice before I take you in. Driver's license and registration. Now."

Without thinking, in my difficult moment of fluster and inability to prove my veracity, I turned inwardly to Ralph and asked him, "Did you know this was possible?"

The cop looked up from his paperwork. "Of course I do, I was the one who told you about it."

An idea developed in my head.

"I wasn't talking to you. I know you knew. You did tell me about it. I was asking someone else."

"On the phone?" asked the cop, unbelieving what he was hearing.

"No, of course not," I said. "My phone is not even on. See for yourself."

He looked down at my phone and took it into his hand. He woke it, touched some buttons, saw nothing of importance, and handed it back to me. He looked into the back seat of my car, down into the darkness of the floor. Satisfied that there was no hidden person in my car he said, "It'd be best if you said nothing. You're beginning to piss me off."

"Ralph, the police officer doesn't believe that I was talking to you."

"Well, what can we do to convince him otherwise?" was Ralph's answer, which I repeated verbatim out loud, making sure that I imitated his Germanic accent exactly.

"I suppose he could just hear our conversation, that's all."

"Won't he still not believe us?"

"But he must believe us. A normal person wouldn't be able to speak to himself like this."

"Unless he was an actor rehearsing his lines out loud."

"You're not helping, Ralph. Just have a regular conversation with me, that's all."

"Now you're putting me on the spot. I have no idea what to say."

This exchange had taken only a few seconds and the cop looked at me as if he were discovering an alien form of life here on earth.

His hand was still out to receive my driver's license and car registration. He was leaving absolutely no room for prevarication.

"Here," I said as I produced the necessary documentation from my wallet. "But this is just half of the story."

"What do you mean by that?"

"This identifies exactly one half of who I am; the other half is left unrecognized, concealed, completely unrevealed."

"Your name is Ricardo Roy Luna. This is your I.D., your photo. That's all I need. Your registration is under the same name. Anything else, anything that is 'completely unrevealed,' you can explain to the judge."

"No, Ralph, I better not say that. He's liable to arrest me."

"Arrest you for what?" asked the cop.

"My friend just called you something bad in French, but I better not translate it. You might get angry."

"I'm pretty angry already. I told you to zip your mouth."

"Zip," I said, and pressed my lips tightly together. But Ralph, who had just called the cop "a buggered little monkey" in French, told me that I should call him, in English, 'a tight-assed dickless wonder." For good measure, he articulated a phrase in German, which I didn't understand, save for the last word, *"Schweinhund."* I laughed and quickly pretended it was a cough. I didn't know Ralph could insult people polyglottaly. I suppose he heard my thought because he responded, "German is so poor in insults that I relish using other languages to cuss people out.

"Well," I thought, quietly, to Ralph, "You shouldn't insult a cop. Cops are out of control in the States."

"What are you doing?" asked the cop.

"Who, me?" I asked him. "What am I doing? I don't know. I thought I was not speaking. What do you think I was doing?"

"I don't know. I could see the whites of your eyes and you were moving your lips."

"Ah, well, I… I was speaking to my friend, but wordlessly. I was thought-speaking to my friend, since you commanded me not to speak. I didn't know my eyes and lips moved when I did that."

"I should take you into the station. Are you on drugs? Are you on medication, or something?"

"I have not been taking any drugs. I've never taken any drugs. But you're right, in a way. The reason why I've never taken any drugs is because my connection with reality has always been very loose. I certainly have never needed anything artificial to disassociate myself from reality."

Ralph breathed into my ear, "That's useless. He's a moron. He doesn't understand a word you're saying. Look at him. He certainly doesn't know what to do with you."

I figuratively brushed Ralph aside so I could address the cop directly. "I never used drugs because I was afraid they would push me into a state of alienation."

That didn't seem to work either.

I tried again: "Drugs would have made me even crazier?"

Mr. Police Officer gave me back my cards along with a

ticket to punish my alleged contravention. "You can explain it to the judge, if you decide to contest it," were his parting words.

After I was back in the car I cried out, "Damn! It's for a hundred and forty-four dollars!"

"Just pay it," recommended Ralph. "The judge might add to it if we go in to speak to her."

"I suppose you're right," I told Ralph out loud. "The world isn't ready for us, Ralph. Each of us alone is passably sane, I guess. But together, you and I are *verrückt, dingues, achusemados,* demented," I added for polyglottal effect. All of a sudden I felt such pity and compassion for unilinguals. There should be an international charity for them, like there are for illiteracy. 'Stamp out monolingualism! Help the ignorant, the poorly educated, the world illiterate. Help train them for a better tomorrow, with better recognition of foreign cultures and respect for alien customs. Teach them another language for a better world and help train world-citizens. Please give generously. Help stamp out parochialism. Unite to end world unilingualism!'

Both Ralph and I sighed at the same time. Those people who didn't understand what parochialism was would prefer to die than to release their small-mindedness from their cold, stiff skulls. I remembered an American family at a restaurant in a small village off the beaten track in Guatemala, asking if there were hamburgers. Even though I was a boy, I realized the inanity of that. Dude, you can eat a sumptuous *tamal* or a beautiful *enchilada* or earth-shattering *huevos rancheros!* You want a hamburger? *Yanqui,* you deserve to stay home!

Like a previous governor from the Bible-belt state of Texas who famously said, when asked if the Bible should also be taught in Spanish, "If English was good enough for Jesus, it's good enough for me!"

Ralph became very interested in my doctoral dissertation. I had written it on the novel by Jean-Baptiste Louvet de Couvray, *Les Amours du Chevalier de Faublas,* which was revolutionary in two ways: its hero was also its heroine, and its numerous editions straddled the French Revolution, 1789-1794, which, after it was all over, had torn asunder the very fabric of French society, had left nothing unaltered, including the calendar, and had exchanged a way of living with another that was no better, and in a way, recycled the old into a new replica that emulated the past. It destroyed the old way of doing things, tried to replace it with weird new schemes, and ultimately self-immolated. In certain ways, the Revolution made things worse. Louis XVI had already outlawed slavery in the French colonies overseas; Napoleon rescinded that enlightened decision and brought slavery back. Popular revulsion against the Catholic Church had stripped it of its political power; the Revolutionaries came up with a new deity, the goddess Liberty, which was to be worshipped above all else. In any case, Louvet de Couvray, who became a Revolutionary himself, wrote about the adventures of his hero, a young aristocrat by the name of Faublas, who, as the Faux Blas that his name suggests, was very unlike his literary predecessor, Gil Blas, a young virile character of the eponymous novel by Lesage. Now here is a picaresque hero who always manages to lead himself out of predicaments by use of his plucky instincts and quick wit! On the contrary, young Faublas always seems to get himself into predicaments, all because he learns to metamorphose himself into a young lady, the better to have access to other young ladies. How better to seduce a girl, than by being a girl! An innocent slumber party that is accompanied by a Trojan horse, this is the stuff dreams are made of, and Faublas never tires of surprising new unsuspecting lasses with his dual nature that he springs on them after they've been lulled by his femininity. A pretty blushing demoiselle who turns into a provocative—and irresistible—young man whose only desire, that of seduction, is quickly consummated.

"We are like Faublas, you and I," said Ralph to me. "Only in this instance we are two men."

"We are also not using our duality in the enterprise of seducing women."

"Because you're not interested in it," he said. "Theoretically, we could."

I found this to be distasteful, especially as he was a married man. I told him so. "You're a married man!" I said.

"Well, yes," he agreed. "But, theoretically, if you seduced a young lady and I came along for the experience, I would not be adulterous. It would be you who would be responsible for the seduction."

"Theoretically, I suppose you would be right," I conceded. "I'm afraid this is something that we won't put to practice. My heart wouldn't be in it. Neither would my dick."

"Don't say never," answered Ralph cryptically. "One never knows one's possibilities; they are not to be limited."

"I believe Nature is the one to do the limiting in this regard," I said to put the matter to rest.

But Ralph hardly ever wishes to put matters to rest. With a chuckle, he said, "It would certainly put a new wrinkle in the term 'ménage à trois,' wouldn't it?"

Ralph could have said something at this stage about how

he had already used my body to make love with his wife, without my knowledge, to say nothing of my approval. But he said not a word. It would be months before we would find out the consequences of his body snatching.

Towards the end of the semester, Bo told me that I had developed a distinctive German lilt to my English.

"What? A German 'lilt'? Don't you mean 'taint'? Are you sure? You really think so?" I asked, alarmed. I wondered if my French had also been adulterated.

Ralph quickly interjected, "Speaking English with a German accent doesn't mean it's a taint, and it certainly doesn't mean it's been adulterated!"

"Well, I'm sorry, Ralph, in this particular case you are wrong, very wrong, just wrong! Accept it! In this case, goddammit, you will not win!"

Both Ralph and Bo were intimidated by my outburst. Neither one said a word while I expostulated.

"I came into this country at the age of five in February of 1960. There were no other Spanish speakers in Hialeah at the time, save for a little Puerto Rican girl at school who was my lifeline. I held on to her as if my life depended on it. I'll never forget her name: Alicia Fuertes. She spoke both English and Spanish equally well, without any sort of an accent in either language. I quickly learned that if I made mistakes in my English, the other little boys and girls in class would call me a spick. How five-year-olds knew to do this, I've no idea. This happened right before the Cuban influx began. Hialeah was an American hick town at the time. Now it's a Cuban hick town.

"Americans are such hypocrites. The say they extol the individual, the one who listens to the beat of a different drummer, the one who follows his own shining star, the one who stands out from the crowd. This is absolute hogwash, as a little five-year-old will tell you. You stand out from the crowd, you're beaten down, disparaged, offended to your very face, then thrown out as a pariah. You follow your own rhythm, you will be insulted, smeared, then ignored, if you are lucky. You speak with an accent, you will be told to get back on your banana boat and go back home.

"At five years old, how did I know that being called a spick was a terrible thing? How I learned to despise that insult! The deprecating tone, the scorn with which it was said, taught me even faster that I had to clean up my pronunciation. I couldn't allow myself to sound different. Later in high school, I learned I had a facility with the pronunciation of French. I was a good mimic, and without much effort, really, I learned French with an accent that was good enough to pass as a Frenchman. It's not just the sounds of the words, I realized, but also the little interjections, the expressions and gestures, all of the cultural differences that go along with learning a language. The French don't start counting on their fingers with the index finger; they put up their thumb first. They don't go "hmm-hmm" for yes or "uh-uh" for no. They utter an elongated and whispered "oui" with an intake of breath, and a brisk "tsk" with a half-turn of the head for the no.

"The French won't despise you for being different; but they will refuse to understand you if you mispronounce their language. And if you pronounce their language badly, they'll even stop paying attention to you. I've seen it with my own students who go to France and can't get anybody to answer their questions or give them directions.

"I take pride in speaking my languages with no accent. I don't want my pronunciation to become adulterated, not in the least altered. I want to pass through society unnoticed, unrecognized as a foreigner. Consider it as a little boy's desire to fit in, in order not to be punished. The truly hard part came later, much later, when I was older and realized I was even more different than most other people. God, but that was hard! It was a completely new exercise in not being noticed. It was making a conscious effort in a perpetual sense that wound up refashioning part of my character, rewiring my personality. I didn't want anybody to know I was gay, even before that knowledge had seeped into my own consciousness. I didn't want anybody to know I was different in that way. In my mind, I was five years old again, as helpless and ingenuous as ever, and my desire to hide what made me different sprang up for the same reason. Not to be punished. Not to be insulted. The more others around me bore the marks of the sissy, those who I supposed were unable to change their ways to hide their feminine gestures, or perhaps they who were the more courageous ones and wanted to exist with audacity right in the face of others, the more they were bullied and called fag and queer, the more entrenched I became in my decision not to be found out. I felt like a victim and I did not wish to be a victim. I did not join in the name-calling, however, refusing to fall into the trap of other little queer boys who, by hurling insults at their more unfortunate brothers, sought to remove any attention focused on themselves. Cruelty was cruelty, no matter what reason caused it to boil over. By remaining quiet, I felt that I had nothing to prove, especially to the bullies, about my apparent masculinity—for I was masculine—and so I didn't need to denigrate others to make myself feel superior to them. I just didn't want to be a victim. In hindsight, I should have bullied the bullies, but asking that of a child is as unfair as it is anachronistic: you can't be ready for something until you are ready for it! Today, of course, I realize that the worst of the bullies were those closet queens themselves, avid to throw the scent off their dubious sexuality. A boy comfortable with his heterosexuality has no need to fear a queer. Why should he? There's no temptation. All he has to say is 'No, thanks' and move on to a girl."

Bo, of course, understood me. Surprisingly, so did the heterosexual Ralph. He said, as I transliterated quietly to Bo, "I've been called 'Kraut' by English speakers and 'Bosch' by French speakers enough times to realize that what you are saying is true. To say nothing of 'Nazi' which is thrown at us wholesale. None of us likes to be pilloried. We all like to fit in. Humanity as such will always cast aspersions to the stranger, the alien, the foreigner. Outsiders are not allowed to fit in, so they band together for comfort, for acceptance. Immigrants are treated with disrespect, with suspicion. Ironically, by the very same people whose ancestors were thus treated just a few generations ago."

Ralph's tone took a sorrowful turn. "I'm sorry, Rick, if my constant association with you is in any way modifying you, the way you speak, the way you think, the way you look at the world—"

"Ralph," I responded before he finished his thought, "You don't have to go that far. It's true that our association together has changed me in certain ways, and that I have learned to adapt to your presence, just as you had to learn to adapt to mine. As a matter of fact, you've had to adapt to a whole new existence, inside a whole new body and proximity to a mind with its own ways of deciphering the world. You now see the world through color-blind eyes! How could we not get each other to change?

It would be impossible not to change. Our proximity is too immediate, too close, too intimate, for it to be otherwise. I just don't want to lose myself entirely in this process, just as you, I'm sure, want to remain autonomous, true to your character, to your ideals, to everything you hold dear and true. Thank god we have similar outlooks, that, as *dix-huitiémistes,* we possess similar values, that we both believe in the Enlightenment, for god's sake, and that, finally, we are both atheists! Can you imagine that a Jesus freak had come to you and was living inside your mind? I would have shot myself in the head just to get him out of there! Can you imagine that a Muslim terrorist had gotten inside your mind! He would have wanted to take over completely, and you would have had to fight back. Who would have won?"

We both turned to look at Bo who looked reassured. "You're both okay, then? I didn't mean to start World War III with a little observation that Rick had a slight German pronunciation, every once in a while, in his English. I don't know about his French. But I take it back. Nowhere in what you just said, Rick, did you pronounce even remotely with a German accent. It was all pure and simple American English. Every once in a while, I might add, you pronounce something with a British accent, especially after we've been watching British programs. I suppose that being a linguist, you pay attention to the nuances of the ways people speak. You are ultra-sensitive to oral expressions and the manner in which they are pronounced, then you incorporate them into your own speech patterns. There's nothing wrong with that. It makes you more internationally-minded. And now, with a German living inside your head, you truly do win the prize."

Both Ralph and I laughed at that. This was the basis of our

camaraderie. We were both highly, heavily internationally-minded. We most probably would have become friends had we met at a convention of linguists or at an antiquarian book fair, in the more usual way of introducing ourselves and shaking hands and exchanging pleasantries. The fact that we met like this, with no mediation, no lacunae, not the tiniest interstice to separate our individual perimeters, meant that we were mentally conjoined twins. Unable to part ways, unable to restore our individual independence, we had to survive together, and, having no other choice, in order to make the best of our imposed connection, we had to remain friends.

Why didn't Ralph and I go to a psychologist? Or a psychiatrist? Or a parapsychologist? Or a priest, as a last resort? Why didn't we seek the help of professionals, before it was too late?

Because we thought that we could take care of the problem, no, not the problem; the *situation,* ourselves. No university diploma that we knew of would automatically enable another person to look into what was happening and offer an explanation as to why it had happened to us, to say nothing of possible solutions. Doctors would have wanted to prod and poke Ralph's body back in France; mental-health professionals would have wanted to prod and poke into my background to see where I had picked up this delusion, this monstrous charlatanism that they never would have believed in the first place. A parapsychologist would have been our best bet, but they labor in a world of undetermined and ambiguous conclusions which cannot, by any means of scientific rigor, be called facts. But teleportation was involved, as, I suppose, a huge dose of possession, and perhaps telepathy and maybe other sorts of mental phenomena unknown to Ralph and me. A priest was out of the question: he would have wanted to exorcise poor Ralph and I would not allow this to take place. My conjoined friend was no demon; on the contrary, he was nice and polite, smart and helpful. Perhaps I wanted to go back to having myself to myself again, but not at the cost of having Ralph yanked out of me and sent to who knows where. If we could be convinced that he would be sent directly back to his body, then, we would agree to a priest's ritual of casting out the interloper. But I would not take the chance, and for this, Ralph was extremely grateful.

I thought that an entomologist might have had some insights into our situation. After all, insects showed all kinds of imaginative ways to get surreptitiously into each other's bodies. The wasps (from numerous hymenopteran families) that lay their eggs inside a caterpillar is an excellent example, for the little wasp babies know what parts to feast on first to keep the caterpillar alive for as long as possible. But this would have been insulting to Ralph, for he was no parasite eating me from the inside out. He was quite harmless, and I'm sure entomology has never heard of a parasite apologizing for its acquisitive behavior. By this time, of course, Ralph had stopped apologizing to me about having shoved his way into my mind, but I remember at the beginning he had voiced his remorse. I told him numerous times that it had not been his fault. I think, in the end, he finally believed me. Coming into me was as complete a surprise to him as it had been to me, perhaps more, since he was the one to have moved through such a distance.

Viruses were a completely different story, however. Viruses

can come into a healthy cell and take over certain parts of it, like maneuvering the DNA mechanism to spit out replicas of itself, instead of more replicas of the cell itself. Then the newly hatched viruses are free to go elsewhere and suffuse new cells with their recombinant DNA. Of course, the victimized cells burst and die in order for the newly replicating viruses to go marching off. If this wasn't a ghastly way to reproduce, I don't know what would! It leaves the cuckoo bird in the dust. This was more like aliens from outer space come to snatch healthy bodies and minds and alter them from within to breed their new offspring. This was just as disgusting, and I didn't entertain these thoughts for very long. Ralph was extremely grateful about my forbearance. Not that I even looked to find out where the entomology department was at my university.

So we went forward, the two of us, marching in unison, glued together with no possibility of finding a solvent to say nothing of a solution to our forced bond. We were adherents of each other, in a new meaning of the word, for struggling against each other would have harmed us both. We had strength in togetherness; apart we would perhaps not be able to survive. Conjoined twins sharing a mind, we dared not find a way to be wrenched apart. Could we survive being severed from each other? Could we endure such an amputation? Neither one of us was willing to find out.

A few days ago, I spoke with my 96-year-old grandmother who lives in Guatemala City. Ralph startled me when he got boisterous in his excitement to hear us speaking in Gkec-chí. I didn't think this was any big deal because Abuelita and I have always spoken in Gkec-chí, but the linguist in Ralph became wildly enthusiastic and after I hung up the phone with Abuelita he wanted to ask me a thousand questions. I explained that Abuelita learned Gkec-chí as a young girl. She moved to Guatemala City in her teens from the highlands where she was born, in Cahabón, a small village in the department of Alta Verapáz where Gkec-chí, one of the Mayan languages, is spoken. Twenty of the approximate seventy Mayan languages are spoken within the borders of Guatemala, and Ralph wanted to find out every last detail. I told him that I spoke Gkec-chí well enough to get by but that I couldn't very well converse about philosophy with it. I let him have access to books published by an uncle of mine, the one who had been murdered, Francisco Curley García, about the Gkec-chí language, its vocabulary and grammar, and another couple of his books about the Gkec-chí culture and legends. I was able to tell Ralph about their cuisine and promised to cook him some Gkec-chí dishes. Ralph had read the *Popol-Vuh* a long time ago, which is accepted as the Mayan bible, containing the genesis myths and all that. It was translated into Spanish from the original Quiché by one of the conquistador priests in the region of Quetzaltenango, the second largest city of Guatemala and the birthplace of my mother who was born there during the time her father was the mayor. But Gkec-chí, a totally different language, has its own set of folklore and myths. I should have realized that Ralph would be interested in the Maya, remembering that one of three extant codices, or Mayan tablet books, is located in Dresden. How it got there, I've never learned. But the fact that only three books escaped the bonfires of the conquistadors is extremely sad. Here was a case where the Spanish foreigners came and, using the regional bellicosity that existed between the Mayan populations who were different even unto their languages, divided them to the point that they were easily conquered. This, in spite of the ridiculously small number of initial conquerors. The usurpers won and attempted to erase everything about the people they had conquered. The very little we still know about the effaced civilization, after five hundred years, is precious, valuable and fascinating. And Ralph latched on to me even more: his professional curiosity could hardly be appeased.

I explained to Ralph that my maternal last name, Xinapó, was from the Gkec-chí expression meaning East Moon, or Newly-Rising Moon, or Young-Sliver-of-a-Moon, but that coming into the United States it had been dropped by a customs official who probably didn't know, and didn't care to know, that Hispanics have two last names, the first one from the father, the second from the mother. That's how I lost my Mayan name and my second 'Moon' and therefore my second set of intertwined DNA strands was completely ignored by my adoptive country. Generations before, people like me were called "half-breeds," as if to deny our totality. The only part that seemed to matter to them was the half that came from white European ancestry. Today, of course, we know that DNA always creates an inseparable whole, and this infusion of totally new DNA strands probably strengthened the tired old European genes. There's always been a family legend of one of our ancestors being an Irishman with blue eyes and red hair who came to Guatemala by way of Belize, which used to be called British Honduras and was settled by British pirates. I suppose the rare blue eyes and the unnerving red hair became sublimated to the dominant chromosomes. They were engulfed and spliced into new strands of creation, a new way of being. I told Ralph that I felt comfortable in my own skin, and happy to know that I was an amalgam of the Old World and the New, of Spanish, Irish, and Mayan stock, of wind-blown ancestors whose fortuitous travels landed them in tropical jungles there to meet the black jaguar and the indigenous shaman whose books they promptly burned, whose children they enslaved, but whose heredity they incorporated into their own offspring, creating new life that was neither foreign nor native, but rather something that was in-between, like a bridge across the gap of time and space.

Ralph couldn't get enough of this. He tore through all my Mayan books, attempting to learn vocabulary by himself. I had to help him with the pronunciation; Mayan has consonant sounds I've never heard anywhere else. He went rummaging through parts of my mind that I thought dormant, for he was creating phrases and inchoate thoughts in this new language. I laughed the day he announced to me: *Laín taquaj jun li caxlanguá!* (I want to eat a tortilla!). I promptly dialed the number of a Guatemalan lady I know in the Redlands who cooks regional dishes for her compatriots, ordering not only tortillas but *frijoles volteados, tamales,* and *chuchitos.* I made *chiles rellenos, atol de elote,* and *horchata* for my German guest. Ralph was thrilled with this new cuisine he'd never tasted. Now he wants to travel to Guatemala. I asked him, before or after Europe? He said that Edmée could come to Miami, then we'd all travel to Guatemala. *¡Ay, ay, ay!* Where would we get the time? I told him I would think about it, and ask Bo. I've never taken Bo to Guatemala. Perhaps it was time.

Something weird and unsettling happened last night, and neither Ralph nor I can explain it. It was a Tuesday night, a night like any other, with nothing different or difficult occurring in our shared life. We had gone out with Bo for Italian, chicken cacciatore, pasta, a little bit of garlic bread, mixed vegetables, two glasses each of a nice Cabernet, no dessert. Bo went to his house to sleep because he had to get up extra early in the morning. Ralph and I went to sleep a little bit late because I wanted to finish a chapter in a book I was reading, which Ralph has been enjoying as well. It is a history book that tells of the incognito trips that royalty sometimes took when they wanted to see other places but didn't want anybody to recognize them, like Peter I of Russia traveling through Europe as Sergeant Pyotr Mikhailov, or Joseph II traveling multiple times as *le comte* de Falkenstein, or the King of Poland, Stanislaw Leszczynski, as *le comte* de Lingen; or Gustav III King of Sweden, as *le comte* de La Haye, and so on. So, nothing unusual happened that night, nothing at all different.

Around half past three in the morning both Ralph and I were fully awake, breathing hard and our heart pounding in our chest. I was in a cold sweat, with Ralph sounding like he was galloping inside my mind. I fumbled for the light switch as I heard someone moaning, realizing almost instantaneously that it was me. With the light on in the bedroom came the realization that we had just had a nightmare. But the abnormal part of it was that we both had the same nightmare. This is the first time, and I hope the last, that this happens to us. We usually sleep at different times, so the fact that we were both asleep simultaneously, and that we had this dream in unison was freakish. What are the chances that two different people will both visualize the same plot of a disturbing dream? Who would have known that we could share a dream? The dream itself was calm, too calm, but surreal as all hell. It still disturbs me when I think of it. Ralph refuses to think about it, saying that it's an omen, an omen sent by whatever power wrenched his consciousness away from his body and dropped him into mine, with a message intended to convey to us that he's slated soon to die.

We dreamt that we were each of us sleeping in the dark on a cot, like a small army cot, alone, all alone, like before, when I was without Ralph. Ralph told me that he had dreamt this very same thing, but that it was he who was all alone on the cot, without me. We each individually saw in our dream a vision that we were sleeping in a big rectangular room filled with other cots arranged in neat rows, a foot apart in either direction, like in an overfilled hospital. When we woke up we were in the dark. We knew that the person beside us was Bo, for me, and Edmée, for Ralph. He, or she, was still sleeping. Behind us we heard voices, so we got up and headed in that direction. There were people milling around an open doorway, with somebody propping it open. On the other side of the doorway, we could see a staircase going up. Somebody was walking up, the others were standing around, looking up with curiosity to where the stairs lead. I came up to the doorway and glanced up. A bright white light seemed to be pouring forth from someplace up the stairs, and I could hear voices, muffled and unclear, from up there. To get a better look, I edged closer to the staircase and some of the voices became clearer, although I could still not perceive a thing because the light was too dazzling. These voices were saying that they didn't want to lose their body. Nobody had told them that they were about to lose their body. A particularly angry man's voice was saying that they, the people who had gone up the stairs, should have been warned, that by going up the stairs they would eventually be losing their bodies, and he had not known to prepare for that. Nobody should be surprised like that, especially for something of so much importance. He must have been an attorney, he was so insistent. I kept expecting him to say next that he was going to sue those responsible for him having to lose his body, and that this alert never appeared in any fine print.

I looked back towards the cots and saw that Bo was still sleeping, but here and there, there were more people waking up. Some just sat on their cots, half asleep, while they decided what to do. Ralph also looked back, independently of me but at the same time as I, to see Edmée still calmly asleep on her cot.

Meanwhile, up the stairs the angry man's voice became pleading and plangent: "Why don't you people understand? I've lost my body! This is not satisfactory! I was not warned. Nobody told me that by going up towards the light I would be losing my body!" He was practically weeping as he realized that it was too late to come back downstairs and regain his body. His body no longer existed.

In my dream came the knowledge that the man was speaking to and pleading with Jesus Christ and that he had been speaking to him for quite some time. The man was trying to convince Jesus that it was not okay that he'd lost his body, that he missed his body a lot, and perhaps he might insist on going back downstairs in order to regain his body. He regretted having gone up the staircase. Jesus seemed to be trying to get this man to understand that things would be much better going into the future without his body, if he'd only give it a chance, for when he'd be in the presence of God, the feeling would be much better than any of the feelings the man felt while he had his body. I understood the man's fear, and the man's regret, at not having his body anymore. How can pleasure, especially sexual pleasure, ever be approximated, or equaled, to say nothing of surpassed, by the alleged ecstasy of being in the presence of God?

I lurked in the shadows next to the base of the staircase. Other people refused to go up as well, but one lady started climbing the stairs tentatively. I certainly didn't want to go up. I looked back at Bo's cot. I would never ever leave Bo. The love I have for and from him is so strong and powerful, so consoling and reassuring, that there is no way I would ever exchange that for a promised eternity of bliss next to God. I'm not sure I trusted Jesus, either; his ideology, to me, has always been unnecessarily intricate, serpentine, and elaborately threatening, what with promises of cannibalism and vampirism and eternal salvation from a sin which was not mine to begin with. I was not buying what he was selling! I was not ready to exchange the gift of human love, with its profusion of feelings and emotions, with its concomitant thrill and balm, for a supposed spiritual rapture that in the end may not live up to its potential. Live forever bathed in divine light? It just didn't sound feasible. As if backing up from a precipice, I, and at the same time, Ralph, returned to the cots and we sat back down, all alone, unaccompanied by the other, next to our beloved. We both had the same thought, that we would wait in the darkness until our beloved woke up. Rattled and afraid, we could only wait. Then we heard a sound like a whooshing rocket and saw a light storm coming from the staircase. Everybody who was on the stairs or near them was being taken up, regardless of where on the staircase they were. I guess Jesus decided to put an end to the quibbling and the kvetching and decided to take the whole bunch up immediately, no explanations, no apologies, no repentance. Whether they were ready to walk up on their own and exchange their physical body for an eternity of bliss—or not—they were spirited away to some other dimension and the whole staircase disappeared. There was nothing left but a gaping hole in the wall. That's when we woke up.

"That was the weirdest dream I've ever had in my entire life!" I said to Ralph as my breathing calmed down.

He agreed. "It was so real! It felt like I was really there, in that room full of cots, next to that staircase."

"But it had to be metaphorical, don't you think?" I asked.

"That's your voice of reason now trying to explain, trying to interpret the dream. I'm not seeing it as metaphorical. It felt real, with so much detail. I felt a slight cool breeze descending from that staircase. Didn't you?"

"Now that you mention it, yes, I did. And the light was not constant, it was diffuse and fluctuating, brightening and waning, varying in strength."

"Yes, and while we could hear people's voices, especially the man who regretted losing his body, Jesus's voice we couldn't hear. We could understand what he was saying, but he had no voice; he was not speaking, but communicating without words."

"You're right. I hadn't noticed that, till now. We couldn't see him, either, since he was too close to the light."

"I think rather he might have been the light," suggested Ralph.

"Possibly. But the light became stronger when the whole thing was sucked up out of sight above us. Then, complete darkness."

"But didn't you notice that there were windows in the big room with all the cots?"

"Yes, yes! I can see them. On the wall opposite the staircase, or rather, where the staircase had been."

"Did you notice, too, that the windows were covered with blinds?"

I closed my eyes the better to see the blinds.

"Yes, they were dark, and they were longer than the windows. They trailed all the way to the ground."

"I think that the blinds were there and they were removable. I think I saw some light behind them."

"Yes, yes, the light of dawn! We could easily have gone over to raise the blinds. Why didn't we do that?"

"Because the sound of all those people being sucked up into space was so awful. You could hear their screams for just a second, and then, nothing."

"That was pretty awful. I was so glad to be sitting next to Bo."

"I didn't see where Bo was. I didn't see where you were, either. I was sitting next to Edmée. I was alone."

"Come to think of it, so was I. You weren't there, or Edmée, either. I suppose we were first-person omniscient dreamers, allocated the same plot, sharing the same perspective. Same story, two different protagonists, as if we were each other's understudies. Weird. But I don't want this to happen again. We both can't fall asleep at the same time."

"I think it was just coincidence that we did. But we'll make it a point for one of us to be awake and vigilant."

"How could we have both been chosen to have the same dream?" I asked.

Ralph answered immediately. "We weren't the ones chosen. It was the dream… The dream was chosen for us, and for us to have it at the same time. What if I had decided to go up the stairs, Rick? What if I had gone up, and you hadn't? I would have been taken away at the end, without a physical body, ready to begin my ethereal existence."

I tried to chuckle to express my disagreement, but it came out like a fake guffaw expressing a high degree of manic hilarity. Still, I tried to comfort my dream partner. "Oh, Ralph, you don't know that. It was just a silly dream. What if it had been the other way around, you had stayed and I had gone up? Does that mean that I would have been taken away, and when you woke up you would have been alone in my body?"

Ralph said nothing, but I could feel his unease at that possibility. I felt his unease and it quickly became contagious. I felt the full thrust of me not existing any more, with Ralph remaining all by himself to animate my body and make decisions for it.

"Don't go there!" Ralph warned me. "I don't think that is possible. Were you to die, I would go along with you, I'm sure of it. This is your body, and I do not want to take over, I assure you. I don't want to remain here by myself! I would be nervous to stay here alone inside your mind. Oh, dear Lord! What are we going to do, what are we going to do?"

"For the time being, nothing, Ralph," I told him. I felt that I had been clobbered, not wholly understanding his comment about being afraid of my mind, but I didn't want him to know I was thinking about it. In his anguished state, he didn't become conscious of my hurt feelings.

"I'm going to make us some tea," I suggested. "I don't want to go back to sleep."

"Neither do I," said Ralph, as he accompanied me into the kitchen. As if he had any other choice.

"What do you want?" I asked.

"Some Darjeeling would be nice."
"Ach, I wanted some orange tea."
"That's okay, too. We'll both have orange tea."

Ever since we shared the same nightmare I've been letting Ralph speak with his wife, Edmée, late at night after I've gone to sleep. It's dawn in France when it's midnight in Miami, so while I slumber, they get to speak. I believe that part of the reason why Ralph wants to speak to his wife, almost on a nightly basis, is because he doesn't want to go to sleep. I believe he is afraid of going to sleep, especially at the same time as I. That nightmare certainly unnerved us! He's more spiritual than I, although I don't think he believes in a Judeo-Christian god. Tell the truth, anybody else is more spiritual than I. He sensed a message in the bad dream, something like 'the bell is tolling for thee' or maybe 'the bell has started tolling for thee.' He's come to the conclusion that it is he whose days are numbered. After all, it's his consciousness that's been squeezed into mine. If anyone goes, it'll be he. I have seniority; he's the newcomer. Can we even talk about squatter's rights here? In any case, I have a tendency to concur with Ralph that if there were one of us to go, it would be he, but I think this as silently as I can since I don't want him to know, but I think he knows nonetheless. I really don't want him to go, at least, not until his body is ready to receive him again. I don't want him to go into a sort of limbo, either. I know that the Catholic Church finally retracted its limbo story, without apologizing, of course. The Catholic Church has never apologized for anything. But the idea of anybody lingering perpetually in a gray area of quasi-non-existence was as sadistic as it was outlandish. One should either exist, or not exist. No median zones of dawdling in nothingness for me. In his book *Many Lives, Many Masters,* Dr. Brian Weiss, who is also from Miami, alludes to a spiritual waiting room where souls go to relax and unwind between lives, but in a sort of irrational and—what is worse for me—ineffable parallel reality. To have the inability to observe empirically whatever world I happened to have around me, not be able to comprehend it and my place in it, and in addition not possess the lexicological ability to determine that reality, would be for me a version of hell. I'm a language teacher; words for me, in many languages, are the essence of my mission in life. I listen to or speak in Standard American English; the whole panoply of signification, connotation, import, and implication are there for me to delve into, to rummage through, including non-verbal hand gestures and facial expressions that are part and parcel of that English. I switch to Standard French, and I begin anew with a completely different system of communication, including—and especially—the non-verbal aspects which are all different. Turning to Castilian Spanish, we come to another completely different system. Languages are as individualistic as people, each with its accompanying utterances and motions, nuances, intonation patterns and pitches, and as we go from one to another we explore all the rich ways of the creation of signs that humans have devised to be able to interpret meanings in order to share our reality with each other and not feel that we are alone. Without this language and the ability to use it, the reality in which we find ourselves remains nebulous, tenuous, phantasmagorical, and surreal. In addition, we feel terribly isolated and alone. I read with great interest Dr. Jill

Bolte Taylor's journey through the experience of a stroke in her book, *My Stroke of Insight,* which begins with the isolation and loneliness that such an event brings.

Edmée reported that there has been no change in Ralph's body. He was still at home since the hospital didn't want anything to do with it. Once all the gastric and nasal tubes were removed, he regained the ability to swallow. Edmée was giving him a protein- and fat-rich concoction of her own making. The doctors apparently were surprised, perhaps even a little annoyed, that the patient had not immediately died, but were unconcerned about readmitting him into their wards, and back into their responsibility. Apparently Ralph had exceeded the time limit of his health insurance. Such arbitrary rules. One's coma may last only a set amount of time and after that, the patient has no right to be cared for at the hospital. Edmée had heard about a sand bed and procured one for Ralph. It is supposed to prevent bed sores. She did have a curious comment which her husband shared with me: she realized that Ralph was no longer snoring. He had always snored, but ever since his stroke, there was no more snoring. Both Ralph and I could not answer that conundrum: why would his snoring have been taken away at the same time as his consciousness?

After mid-terms, but way before finals, I noticed Ralph was growing taciturn and melancholy. His excitement with Gkec-chí died away, he wasn't helping out in classes, and had no say in what I had for dinner. "Whatever you want," he would mutter after I asked him. I stopped asking him.

One morning he didn't make himself known for a long time. I had had my coffee, my blueberry muffin, I had checked my emails, taken a shower, and, at last, when I was getting into the car he finally spoke.

"You forgot the French 102 quizzes by the copy machine."

"Ah, *merde!*" I said, and rushed back into the house to retrieve them. "Thanks for that," I told him. "I would have been in deep trouble later."

"The students would have loved it."

"Not the two or three who like taking quizzes. The ones who always get the best grades. They would have been disappointed."

After I had started the car and was off to school, I asked Ralph, "Where were you this morning? You sleep in late?"

"I was awake. Just quiet. Sometimes I feel like being quiet."

"Really?" I asked, genuinely surprised. "You could have fooled me!"

"Whatever do you mean?"

"Ralph, you're one of those people with the gift of gab. You can say anything to anybody, and get them talking as well. I'm the one who is quiet. At parties I don't say a word."

"You don't go to parties," responded Ralph, as if I should know that better than he.

"Of course, I don't. I hate parties. I never know what to say to people I barely know. You, however, are never at a loss for words. You gab, gab, gab, and don't ever seem to get tired of it. Why do you think I notice when you don't say anything?"

"Well, don't I have the right to stay quiet sometimes? And we just passed a cop. You should just think your responses to me, not speak them out loud. Your habit of speaking to me has already gotten us in trouble once."

"But it's easier to say things out loud. I wasn't made for

telepathic communication. It's words that give me the meaning I want to convey. Thought statements are an oxymoron. Without a form to put your thoughts in, they become… they become large, messy, with expanding and relaxed borders, borders that leak into other thoughts, then communication becomes vague, not precise enough. I prefer enunciated words, utterances that—wham!—slice the silence and sculpt my meaning. I like that. I like choosing the right word for the right meaning. I say what I want, I want to say it the way that I want."

"I suppose I know what you mean. But I have no choice. If I want to use your mouth and larynx, you have to be asleep, so I can never 'speak' to you. If I want to communicate with you, I can only do it telepathically."

"Well, sorry about that. I'll try to be more of a telepath with you. Does that word even exist, telepath? Well, it does now."

I frowned in frustration. "See what I mean?" I continued to 'think' to him. "That 'Well, it does now.' It felt more like 'Well, from now on it will.' Don't you think so?"

"I got the gist. That's what is important."

"Ah, of course. I'm sure Flaubert and Tolstoy felt that it was the gist that was important."

"Sarcasm won't work with me. I mean to say that the gist is adequate for everyday types of conversation. Of course it is not at all sufficient for the 'high art' of literature. There, of course, your vocabulary, your syntax, everything in your arsenal becomes important. Still, how many ways are there to say, 'Beautiful lady, your lovely eyes make me want to die of love'?"

I started to laugh. "Well, you could say it like this, 'Your lovely eyes, beautiful lady, of love make me want to die.' "

"I think I prefer," Ralph went on, " 'Lovely lady, to die of love make me want your beautiful eyes.' "

"No, no, no, this is better: 'Of love to die, lady beautiful, make me your eyes lovely want.' "

"Here is the best way, I'm sure you'll agree: 'Your lovely eyes of love want to make me, beautiful lady, die.' "

"Are you mad! This is the way to say that, and I'm final in this. It's 'Eyes of your love make beautiful to die, lovely lady to want me.' "

I'm surprised we weren't stopped by the police. The car was swaying in its lane so erratically because laughter was so much roaring, from the road it kept my eyes, stomach muscles spasming with pulsating contractions, mouth open with mirth, keeping melancholy at the back, in the dark, in the subliminal viscosity bordering awareness.

Ralph told me about a project that he had been working on before his stroke and that had only recently come back to his memory. It was a translation of *The Song of Roland* into German.

My first reaction was a stifled laugh. We were sitting at the breakfast table enjoying a blueberry muffin and a cup of strong, black coffee.

"I'm sorry, Ralph," I said out loud to him. "I just have never thought about *La Chanson de Roland* existing in German."

"It exists already, in many translations. My publisher and I thought that a new, more modern translation was in the offing."

"In the offing, huh?"

"Why, yes. Every generation or two needs a new version. *Beowulf* keeps being translated into modern English."

"Funny you should mention that. I can definitely see *Beowulf* in German. But I just can't see *Roland* in it."

"Is this another one of your prejudices against the German language?"

"No, no, no, Ralph! Not at all! It's just that, I mean… How do you deal with the rhyming alexandrine couplets and the hemistich and, most importantly, the non-stressed French syllables?"

"The same way you deal with all translations. As best as you can! You're there to mediate the language, to interpret the meaning. On the one hand you represent the author and you stand in for his original intentions, but at the same time you recast them in a new voice, in a new language. I mean, look at the word: *translatus* in Latin refers to the action of transfer, of 'carrying across.' At the same time one worries about keeping the writer's artistry intact. I know it is especially difficult for poetry, but these old sagas weren't that complex. I was three-quarters done with it. And I was going to be paid a handsome sum for it, too!"

"So, finish it!"

"I beg your pardon?"

"Go ahead and finish it. Edmée will turn in it for you, saying that she found it among your papers. Your publisher should still pay for the work, don't you think?"

"Yes, I think he would, I think he would at that. You have convinced me, Rick. I think I shall finish it. At nights when you're asleep. Ha! You'll be making money while you sleep, you realize that?"

"But that'll be your money, Ralph. I don't want to take your money."

"Well, I still would like to compensate you for the trip to

Europe. Getting the tickets at the last minute must have cost a pretty penny."

"Well, it was necessary for us to go when we did."

The next time Ralph spoke with Edmée on the phone, he asked her to scan and send through his email account all the pages he had already done for the translation of *Rolandslied*. The following day we received them before dinner, and after I had gone off to bed, Ralph spent the night continuing his translation. In a fortnight it was done, in a month Edmée had received the fee from the publisher, and part of it sailed across the Atlantic to land in my bank account.

"That was great!" exclaimed Ralph. "We should do it again! Can you believe that I am writing posthumously!"

"You are not writing posthumously, Ralph! You seem to neglect the fact that you are not dead!"

"Well, I think I'm brain dead."

"Well, that's a matter of opinion," I offered.

"What do you mean?"

"Nothing, Ralph. It was a lame joke."

"Oh, I see. Ha, ha! I get it. Yes, I got it!"

I couldn't help laughing in turn.

But such were the circumstances that gave birth to Ralph's second profession. By night, he became a translator, a novelist, and an autobiographer. He started to write his memoirs, albeit in semi-fictionalized form, as one is wont to do. We would have breakfast together during which he would tell me about his writing. I would tell him about my activities slated for that day, not that my schedule changed that much. But during the next couple of months, I stopped hearing from him as much, especially in the morning, considering he was tired after spending a whole night rummaging through his memory and recomposing his past. For days at a stretch, such was his silence that Bo and I felt that we had gone back to the time before Ralph had burst into our lives. The German professor-cum-memoirist would be gone for whole swaths of time, and Bo and I felt that we were alone again.

The exercise of reconstituting the past was of further benefit to Ralph: he became much calmer and was even able to achieve a modicum of happiness, given the circumstances. For those few weeks we all enjoyed the lull of peace, the satisfaction of work, and the reprieve from depression that only writing can bring. Of course, this all came crashing down the moment we found out that Edmée was pregnant. I am so glad it happened after my semester was over. I couldn't have dealt with the pandemonium the news provoked at home together with final exams. It did, however, cause a huge revision of our vacation plans, for instead of going to spend time with friends in Connecticut, we had to fly back to France. I love France, of course, even going there twice in one year. But I've never had to go to France to confront such an intricacy of family drama and accompanying complexities that, to my knowledge, have never existed before.

Edmée decided to tell us the happy news through an email she sent to Ralph.

Cher Ralphie, it said. «*Il faut que je te voie d'urgence. En personne. Je suis enceinte. Ne t'en fais pas, bien sûr que tu en es le père. Dis à tes amis ce que tu veux, mais dis-leur qu'il faut que tu viennes sur-le-champ.*» In English: "I have to see you urgently.

In person. I'm pregnant. Don't worry, of course you're the father. Tell your friends whatever you want, but tell them that you must come at once."

R alph discovered Edmée's email in the middle of the night. It wasn't necessary for him to wake me up; he began such a clamor that the ghosts in the rafters would have been awakened.

"Nein, nein, das is nicht möglich!" he was exclaiming. (That much I can understand: No, no, that is not possible!) I believe that in his mind he was also running, like a man who smells smoke or who feels an earthquake and starts running for the exits. Sadly, he only had the space inside my head in which to run.

"Was ist los? Was ist los?" I asked him, fearing that maybe he had reverted to understanding only his native tongue. (What is wrong? What is wrong?)

"Edmée... Edmée..."

My heart was in my throat. Something had happened to Edmée! She was sick! She was dead!

"The email," Ralph said. "The email... Look at the email!"

I looked, and I understood.

I was aghast. We were aghast. I was the most aghast. What was I going to tell Bo?

How could that have happened?

What had we done? This was a collaborative project; I didn't do it alone. I didn't do it at all! I was completely guiltless of an action that was done through my body, but not with my assent, not even with my acknowledgment. Yet the law said that ignorance was no excuse. What bloody mess had we gotten ourselves into? How did this happen, goddammit?

Even though I didn't say this last question, just thought it, Ralph answered it anyway.

"In the same old usual way that such things happen."

"What do you mean, Ralph. Did you... Did you... My God! You took my body out for a spin, didn't you?"

"What do you mean for a spin? What is a spin? Oh, Lord, how can this be? Edmée is pregnant. She's pregnant!"

"Through *my* body!" I yelled at him. "You used my body for this, for this..."

"Yes, I know! I know! I was the one who was there!"

"But you didn't have my permission! I did not do it, I couldn't do it! I would not have been able to do it! Only through your mind could I have done it. Edmée is beautiful and all, but I couldn't have done it!"

"Of course, you didn't do it. You weren't even there. You were asleep, in another dimension! I was in control of your mind, Rick. *Es tut mir leid!* I'm so sorry, so very sorry. I... I... I suppose I thought that you wouldn't mind! I didn't know that this would be possible, that I... that we... that you could father a child!"

"I'm gay, not sterile!" I yelled back. "You willfully purloined my body and used it for a purpose in which you had no right to engage. And how did Edmée ever think the two of you would get away with this? I am not her husband! How could she have gone to bed with me?"

"With her eyes closed. I was speaking to her in German, and I was mentioning things only we could understand. She was convinced that I was still alive and that I was speaking through you. The rest was just physicality, and I'm sure I made love to her my own old way, not yours. I don't even know how you make love, what tricks you use–"

"Tricks? Tricks? What are you talking about?"

"I don't know! I don't know what you like to do… In any case, she was convinced that it was me, me, her own husband, and not you. You didn't even come into the picture. Well, in a manner of speaking, perhaps you did, at the end… You were just the body that delivered me into her arms. For that I will be eternally grateful. I had another chance to be with my wife. I love her so much. I had missed her so much. To have that gift of holding her again in my arms, to make love to her, to feel at least for a moment that everything was okay, that I was there beside her. Rick, you must understand that your generosity allowed us to be together once more. I thank you for this. I thank you from the bottom of my heart."

I had calmed down for I understood Ralph. I did, however, let out one final blast: "Well, it wasn't just once, was it?"

"No, Rick, it was four times. Four times of bliss, of union with the one I love. Imagine if you had had another chance to be with Bo, whom you love."

"You're right. You're right. I wouldn't have been able to resist it, either. There was a way, there was a chance, you took it. I understand. And I forgive you. As a matter of fact, there is nothing to forgive you about. It was completely natural what you did. I would have done the same thing."

If there were any way that Ralph and I could embrace inside my head, we did. He was my brother, almost like being myself in another avatar but a simultaneous one.

"We just have to figure out the legalities now," I told him.

"The legalities?"

"Yes. What are the legal ramifications of this? Edmée is going to have a baby. Is the baby considered to be yours, or mine?"

"Why can't we say that the baby will be ours?"

"Ours, like, Edmée's, yours and mine?"

"Yes! These days they have surrogates, and babies born from petri dishes, and semen being frozen for decades, and fathers having babies posthumously. There are so many new and wondrous possibilities these days, we just figured out a new way to do this, and frankly it feels quite natural. Can't a baby have two fathers? In this case, ha ha!—the two fathers are not rivals. On the contrary, they're bosom buddies. Mental buddies. Joined at the brain, if I may say. You just thought this a moment ago. We're like brothers, you and I. Remember the Italian castrato, who fell in love with a woman and married her? Well, it was his brother who impregnated his wife. We all find ways to love. Sometimes these ways are not average or common-place. But they work just as well. We can say that I am the father and that you are the godfather. That way, you and I will be forever joined in a spiritual sense."

I telepathed an acknowledgment of my acquiescence.

Ralph continued, "I am at peace, suddenly, with all this. I think it was meant to be. There will be a little being left after I'm gone. This baby is a part of my legacy, and he or she will continue after I'm gone. We have no clue as to how all of this will end. If my body dies, will my mind cease to exist as well? If my body, and brain, recuperate, will my mind, or my soul, or whatever you want to call it, will it reenter into its physical domain? Or is it doomed to die anyway? For how long can a body exist without its mind? And vice versa?"

"Edmée needs you right away."

"Yes, I know. But only you and Bo can make that decision."

"It's not a difficult decision to make, Ralph."

In two days the three of us were on a plane back to France. On the brighter side, we only needed but two seats. That's a good way of saving money. Take your friend on a piggy-ride inside your mind. The question remains, however. How do you reconstitute your friend after you've reached your destination?

I t was raining in Paris when we touched down. Not the fast and furious way we get in Miami, but the paltry, long-lasting way of northern Europe. Overcast skies, cold and foggy air greeted us, with our breath adding to the fog. Bo and I didn't even own coats of sufficient force to deal with this, just a couple of impermeable jackets in tropical colors.

From Charles de Gaulle airport we rented a car and drove immediately to Normandy. The tiny village of Nonant looked dreary as if covered by a pall, with all the trees looking dead and the lawns in front of houses looking tattered in their sogginess.

As soon as Edmée opened the door of her parents' small vacation house, she burst into tears. Both Bo and I hugged her trying to assuage her sobs, but to no avail. In-between huge rifts in her language, she spoke to us in French, which did Bo no good, but I translated for him.

"She wants to see Ralph right away."

The ever practical Bo answered, "Can't we at least get these suitcases out of the rain?"

I helped him bring them into the house. Edmée and I went to sit on the couch in the living room, and I sat back on the cushions, ready and willing to take a nap. But Edmée's huge damp eyes on mine, her hand on my arm thinking that I had

already fallen asleep, her soft voice calling out, "Ralphie...
Ralphie?" made sleep flee rather than come closer. I asked her
for a glass of Calvados.

"I need to relax," I told her.

"Yes, of course, right away."

While she went into the kitchen, Bo sat down on the space
she had just vacated. He put his own hand on my arm and bent
over to give me a deep lingering kiss.

"Do you want me to stay here, or shall I make myself scarce?"

"No, no, please stay here. I want you to be a witness. I don't
want my body used for just anything, you know. It's still my
body. I'm sorry, Ralph. I don't want you, or Edmée, to be taking
leave of your senses. A little decorum here, please. Things are
complicated enough."

Ralph spoke to me, which I transliterated immediately to Bo,
"I just want to tell her what you and I decided back in Miami.
That I'm the father of the child, but that you'll be the godfather."

"That's fine," I said to Ralph. "I just don't want any more
touchy-feely between the two of you, you know? Hugs are fine,
but clothing will not be coming off."

Edmée came back from the kitchen with three glasses of
Calvados. Bo rose to yield the spot back on the couch to Edmée
and took one of the glasses. Edmée gave me mine.

Realizing the momentous occasion, I said, "To friendship,
and to family!"

Edmée burst into tears again, but raised her glass courageously
to her quivering lips and drank with us. The Calvados darted a
trail of vivid warmth down our throats and esophaguses.

"Good stuff!" I said. "This will do it, I think!"

I gulped the rest of the drink down, and reclined on the
couch. I thought of the importance of Ralph and Edmée

speaking directly to each other, but changed my thought patterns in order to clear my mind, intent on becoming sleepy. I thought of mountains and lakes, with a Brahms lullaby soothing the soaring landscapes, quelling the nerves, dispelling the stress, as if I were a hawk adrift among the clouds.

I must have fallen asleep after a few minutes because I remember nothing after that. It was Bo who filled in the lapsus for me afterwards. But he could only tell me very little. Apparently, Ralph and Edmée preferred to speak French and German to each other, so he was at a great disadvantage. Physically, they did nothing, save for sitting on the couch in front of each other, executing a few hugs and performing a few kisses. At one moment towards the end of their conversation, which lasted about half an hour, Ralph took Edmée's face in his hands, and with great passion and exuberance, accompanied his words with kisses that he planted on her forehead, her cheeks, and her mouth. Edmée was laughing and crying at the same time.

Ralph left Edmée to go wake me up, and the first thing he told me as I came back to reality was, "Thank you, Rick, thank you so very much! Edmée and I have decided what is best for us under the circumstances."

As I heard Ralph's voice within me, I saw Edmée and Bo looking at me with anticipation. I nodded at them but raised a hand to indicate that I needed a few moments.

"Yes, Ralph, go ahead," I said out loud so that they would understand that he was speaking to me.

Ralph continued, "We have decided to leave my body here, in the care of a fulltime live-in. Edmée needs to be close to me, close to my mind. She is going to accompany us back to the States."

"As what?" I cried out. "A tourist?"

"She needs to be with me, Rick."

I realize that telling him that his wife needed to be with his body was irrational. Ralph's body was like an apartment with no tenant. I looked at Edmée who wore an expression of hope that I would agree to this idea that she follow us back home. After I told Bo what these people wanted he looked worried. I was worried, too. What about our privacy? Having Ralph inside my head had been complex enough, but now there would be a woman living with us, physically. And speaking about physically, what would there be to stop them from using my body in a carnal way again, without my knowledge, without my permission? Bo, I'm sure, was also thinking the same thing. He wouldn't want a lover who was, like, rented out for the evenings! Speaking about being unfaithful! I couldn't guarantee to him that I would be faithful. And being unfaithful with a woman was adding insult to injury. My initial reaction to Ralph's request was to say no, no, a thousand times no. This was way past complex, this was way past difficult; this was borderline psychotic. It was impossible! I had dissociative identity disorder, which might be permanent; I had multiple avatars that could intercommunicate; I had alternate consciousnesses coming in and out of my mind, during some of which I got amnesia, and during this amnesia my body was used for things of which I was completely unaware. What if Ralph decided to become a murderer or a bank robber or a… or a politician? I would have no control. I felt I was out of control already.

Edmée and Bo continued to look at me expectantly.

Bo asked, "Is Ralph still talking to you?"

"No, he isn't," I replied. "The thoughts I'm having all by myself are so terrible that he has probably gone to the complete opposite side of my mind from where I am."

Bo scrunched up his eyebrows in that handsome way of his.

"I am out of control, Bo, baby," I said. "I can no longer control my mind, and I cannot say that I am in complete control of my body. I'm losing myself in all of this. I am dissipating. I am dissolving, dwindling away, and I don't know where I am. I no longer feel whole. My totality is in tatters. Where is the rest of me?"

I looked at Edmée. "Edmée, you are pregnant with my child. I know that it wasn't me that you made love to, but it was my body nevertheless. Your husband used my body to do something that I could not have done myself. He usurped me. Like a hijacker taking possession of a plane to do something it was not intended to do. You, too, should have known better. You shouldn't have used me like that."

"I know, I know!" cried Edmée emphatically. "And Ralph knows it, too. We shouldn't have taken your body without your knowledge. But, but I saw my husband again in front of me. I thought he was gone forever, but he appeared for an instant before me and when he embraced me he spoke of his love for me, for his desire for me. He told me he missed me. He used the words only my husband could use. They weren't your words. You weren't there. Maybe your body was there, but you weren't. I made love to my husband, not to you. And my husband was able to make love to me. You say that you don't know if you would have been physically, or emotionally, able to make love to me. Perhaps... But that is a moot point. It wasn't you I made love to. It was my Ralphie, my husband, my soul mate. We are sorry to bring complications to you. You didn't ask for any of this, I know. But we didn't either. We were not in control when Ralphie was taken halfway around the world. To Miami, of all places. Why did he land there? Why was it you who was chosen for this enigmatic transplant? We don't know the answers to any of these questions. All I know is that you hold Ralph in your head the way that I hold Ralph's baby in my womb."

This thought hadn't occurred to me. Neither had it occurred to Bo who looked at Edmée as if she were out of her mind.

"Yes," she said. "Ralph is inside your head and his baby is inside me. How about that for nesting boxes?"

"Nesting boxes?" I asked.

"Yes, like a bird who makes her nest in which to place her eggs where they can be safe, where they can be nurtured, where they can hatch. Then the little birds can be looked after, and from this nest they can fly away. My baby will fly away in five more months. Perhaps Ralphie will fly away from you just as soon, maybe sooner. You have been looking after him all this time, otherwise you would not have been helping him, otherwise you would never have even met me. You could have gone to the psychiatrist for drugs or therapy or... or... I don't know! Voodoo or something, to get rid of Ralphie at the very beginning. But you didn't. Your humanity made you accept him and help him. Please, Rick, you must continue to help him still. You can't give up on him now, and you can't give up on us. We are all in this together."

She took Bo's hand in hers, then mine, and brought them all together.

"We were chosen for this bizarre event, and we are all living it together. We cannot separate now. Please Rick, please Bo, please let me go back with you to Miami, so I can be with Ralphie, just for a little bit, just until the baby is born. I... I..."

She began to weep again and covered her face with her hands. After a while, she spoke again. "I have a suspicion that something is going to happen when the baby is born. Something is going to happen to my husband. I don't know what it is. I don't want to think about it. But his child will be born, and I don't think that Ralph's body can survive much longer. His muscles have grown weaker and weaker, he is thinner... Well, come see for yourselves."

Bo and I followed her to the bedroom in which Ralph's body lay in coma. We were shocked at the difference of what a few months had wrought on his physical existence. The atrophy of his muscle tissue was visible as was the thinness of his body. In addition, Ralph was as white as the sheets covering him. His skin had a dry, waxy look. His eyes were sunken, his lips recessed, showing his teeth, like a sinister grin. From within me I heard a weeping. Ralph was weeping for his ravaged body.

I turned away so he could no longer see.

"Ralph," I told him. "Your body is not being used. It's wasting away. How could we find a way for you to get back to it? Bo, are you listening? Certainly medicine, or psychiatry, can do something. This cannot be irreversible!"

Bo said in his calm, soothing bedside manner, "This cannot be possible, and yet, when the evidence is this incontrovertible, one has to accept that it happened. What we are dealing with here is not a matter of medicine or psychiatry. It's more a matter of religion and spirituality. We are delving into the murky world of the unknown, and the unknowable. However..." He turned to Edmée to speak to her. "However, we must have Ralph on daily physical therapy in order for his muscle tone to recuperate. He also needs more nutrition. I am sorry I didn't mention any of this when we were here the last time. I thought Ralph's doctors would have put him on a regimen."

"Ralph's doctors abandoned him without mercy," Edmée

answered bitterly. "The caretaker we leave with him will have to be a physical therapist."

She looked at us. "Or I shall do it, if I remain with him."

Bo and I exchanged glances. Without words we realized that we needed to continue helping this man and his wife. What if it had happened to us? Bo nodded his head, as if to say, let's do it, let's follow this story to its last event.

I said to Edmée, "Okay, Edmée." To Ralph I asked, "Ralph, are you there?"

"Yes," came the response. "I'm here."

"Edmée can come with us. It'll be easier to ask for a tourist visa, then in three months we'll have it extended. But six months is the limit. The baby will have been born by then, and, if Edmée's intuition is right, something might resolve your situation. At least, that's what we're all hoping for. For you to be reunited with your body. Perhaps. For the first time in my life I'm thinking about what is destined to be. Destiny had you brought to me, for safekeeping. I shall keep you safe for as long as I can. What has destiny to decide in the time to come? We cannot even surmise, and there is nothing to analyze for none of this is akin to science. It is all conjecture; it is the biggest mystery of the world and our place in it is an enigma with no explanation and no solution. Some turn to religion, but I cannot. The minutely arcane dogma stop me. No one can know the mechanism of destiny. But even if it is coincidence that rules it, all we can do is wait patiently to see what will come to pass for us. I am sure, however, that if we stand up to it together, joined by our mutual concerns and our mutual love, we will be able to confront, perhaps to accept, whatever may come our way."

Edmée's eyes shone through her tears of joy. Bo's eyes looked as if they had a sheen to them. As for me, I felt tears dripping down my nose and cheeks.

Here we were. Four people, soon to be five, joined by tragedy, connected by destiny, united by volition and courage. Strength in numbers, power of the team, all the dry old platitudes came to mind. Their banality spoke of their veracity, and we needed to cling to that, for there was no other way.

PART 3

We found an ideal caretaker for Ralph. It was the mother of a neighbor of the Ralphs from Regensburg, a retired nurse who knew how to give physical therapy. She had just moved from Auvergne to spend her retirement closer to her daughter, a chemist at a Swiss drug company with branch offices in Normandy. The mother had not yet found her own apartment and was therefore glad she could stay in the Ralph's home for no rent, in exchange for taking care of Ralph.

Meanwhile, the U.S. government gave Edmée a tourist visa without any problem. After a few days, we were all able to fly back together to Miami.

I still had a few days to relax before the new semester started. Bo went back to his regular schedule. Edmée, I could tell, tried to keep a low profile, staying in the guest bedroom for hours, until I told her that she should feel comfortable enough to have run of the whole house.

At that, she set up a frenetic activity in the kitchen, cooking dinner for Bo and me every night, until we told her that we also liked going out to restaurants. Of course she would come with us.

For all intents and purposes, Bo and I had gone to France to bring back a woman. A pregnant woman, to be sure. Our friends were stymied. They didn't know what to think of our situation. We just said that Edmée was a very good friend of ours, and that she wanted to visit Miami. Had they really been on the lookout, they would have realized that Edmée hardly ever left the house, except in the evenings when she accompanied us to dinner. We rented her a car at the very beginning, but she wasn't using it, so we gave it up. Every once in a while, I would invite Edmée to accompany me to the college, especially on those days when Ralph was scheduled to substitute for the German teacher. She loved those times because she could see her husband in action once again. Of course, I would be asleep, resting in some corner of my mind.

In the end, I had to trust the two of them at nighttime, hoping that they would be good and not abuse my body. But if there was any hanky-panky, I doubt I would have been able to know anything about it. I tried not to look too hard at my penis in the mornings, but as far as I could tell, everything was always nice and tidy. I asked no questions. In the end, I came to the conclusion that their physical cavorting with my body, if it were indeed taking place, did not diminish me in any way. I looked upon it as having been a sperm donor. I had given of myself to make another couple happy. I just wished that the legal entanglements would not become convoluted. It was nobody's business, anyway. It was a mutual agreement among four consenting adults, although one of them had been asleep and the other one completely ignorant. I was sorry to have brought Bo into this mess, but he was very understanding and very helpful. He was such a mensch, and I loved him so.

Bo and I had been thinking about giving up our separate houses and building ourselves a new one in which we could live together all the time. Of course, with Edmée staying with us, to say nothing of Ralph, we had to put our plans on hold. It would only be for a few more months. The baby would be born sometime in the spring, a couple of months before my summer vacation. We had plenty of time to greet the new baby, my godchild, stepchild, half-child, surrogate child, whatever the heck it was going to be, and see that Edmée was in a good place before she went back home to Europe. She still didn't know if she was to take up residence in their house in Regensburg or go back to Normandy. It would be difficult to move Ralph's body to Germany. In any case, there was plenty of time to think about the future. There were hundreds of decisions to be made, but they could be made only one by one.

The naming of the baby was rapidly decided. Once we found out that Edmée was carrying a boy, she said that his name would be Richard Beau Ralph, in honor of his two sponsor fathers. She said that it was Ralph's idea to name him after us. He would not have wanted to name his son after himself since he hated his own name, Theophilus, "beloved of God," especially considering he was an atheist. We were honored, and realized that we were very excited about having progeny. Bo and I couldn't have our own children just by ourselves, but this method that we had cleverly devised could very well work out. We started an education fund for little Richard Beau Ralph, just in case he decided to go to school in the States. We wondered what he would call us. Dads? *Père* and *Vater?* Uncle Rick and Uncle Bo? And what would he call Ralph? How would he even get to know Ralph? If an adult has problems recognizing the duality of shared personalities, how would a child deal with it? In order to even speak to his father, I would have to be asleep, and therefore not a participant. We decided to use our languages as demarcation points of our different personalities. Bo and I would always speak in English to our collaborative son; Ralph would always speak in German. Edmée would speak in French. That way he would always know who was who. People eventually sort out the identities of identical twins. Our son would sort out the two personalities that lived inside my head. At least, that was our hope.

We received copies from the German publishers of Ralph's translation of *La Chanson de Roland* into German, *Rolandslied*. It was a handsome volume. The critics were calling it an inspired interpretation. I, of course, couldn't read it, but as I leafed through it, I again recognized, and appreciated, the fundamental duality of the tale. The Christians, lead by Charlemagne, constituted only one half of the story. The other half was composed of a completely parallel world, the Saracens, the Muslims, also called the pagans by the Christians. The Christians, in turn, were the non-believers, according to the Muslims. But both halves were equal and balanced each other like identical weights on a scale: both groups had their kings, Carlomagno and Marsile, who both had nephews, Roland and Aëlroth, and both had horses with names, and even swords with names. Carlomagno's sword, Joyeuse, held a relic in its pommel: the point of the Roman lance that pierced Jesus's flank. An archbishop, Turpin, accompanied the Christians; an imam accompanied the Saracens. Of course, in this war the heathens didn't stand a chance. Not only were they not like the Christians, courageous and upright (they were devious and felonious), but they could not be victorious since they did not have God on their side. The cowardly and sadistic dark-skinned heathens had to be routed in the end, and routed into oblivion. Either that or have them convert to Christianity.

Why couldn't the two groups have coexisted side by side? They had a whole swath of the continent in which to live together. In Alexandria, three groups had coexisted. No, four! The Christians, the Muslims, the Jews, and the Greek pagans. For a couple of centuries all lived in peace, until the archbishop deemed that the Jews had to go. Damn! So many calamities in history have been due to archbishops. Cardinals and popes also have their share of crimes against humanity. Imams, too, have blood on their hands.

We so quickly fell into such a routine that it had everybody feeling that our lives were a bit soporific. We were all taking naps all the time. I needed to take frequent naps to allow Ralph and Edmée time to interact. They were going to have a baby! They had lots of things to plan, many details to figure out.

The wait did take its toll on us. Without counting having to wait for Christmas or my birthday when I was a kid, I can assert with veracity that I've never waited for anything for so long! Five months is a long time. But with the cyclical semester system, one learns to live for the mid-terms, then the second half of the term, then final exams, over and over and over again. Embedded within the framework of the beginning French language classes, there was time travel: we went from the Present tense to the Past tenses, to the Future tense, picking up vocabulary and parts of speech as we went along. In the first Survey of French Literature class, we went from Medieval to Renaissance to Classical Age like clockwork. Ralph gave two lectures this semester, one for the Medieval poets and the other for Montaigne, a Renaissance man whom he loves so much. His main theme for Montaigne was that the philosopher from Bordeaux wrote his essays so that they would stand in for him, the man. The œuvre becomes the corpus which memorializes the man forever. Montaigne was always so preoccupied with his faulty memory and his uncertain legacy that his remembering became his re-membering, like a man trying to stitch up his life, and his limbs, into a coherent whole. The class loved that lecture. I wished I could have told them who had really given it to them.

As Spring approached, we became restless. The sun rose and set, the moon went through her cycles, but we were all attuned to the progression of a fetus who grew and grew to such proportions that little Edmée looked ready to pop. She waddled when she walked, and spent much of her time seated in the living room with a book in her hand. She was going through my library at an alarming rate.

I was never happier to have as a mate a physician. I do not know why everyone doesn't choose a medical doctor as a spouse. His care and concern for Edmée were such that I though that he considered himself the father of the child. I found it excellent that this little boy was going to have three fathers. Three separate minds to help guide him along in life. Bo and I started talking that perhaps Edmée wouldn't have to leave Miami immediately once little Richard Beau Ralph was born. Rearing a child was a collective effort, and Bo and I could certainly be of assistance to Edmée, especially at the beginning of the tyke's life.

The government of the United States proved that it is not always friendly to its citizens, even less so to foreign visitors. We tried to have Edmée's tourist visa extended for another three months, but our local civil servants created such a convoluted muddle of our simple request, that in the end it was decided to send Edmée back to France for a week or two and return with a new visa. It took almost a full month before she could return. By that time, we were sure she would have the baby on the plane, but she managed to stretch her pregnancy out to the full term, and on the first day of spring plus a day, Richard Beau Ralph came into his independent existence.

He looked exactly like me.

Dear *Gott im Himmel*, he was me in miniature. Same mane of hair which comes down so close to our eyebrows that we hardly have any forehead. Same small brown eyes, big nose and thin lips. Poor thing. But on him it all looked really cute: he looked like one of those Scandinavian troll dolls, only with jet black hair.

"I hope you're not too disappointed," I told Edmée.

"No, are you kidding?" she answered with mock offense. "He is absolutely adorable!"

Bo gave his opinion: "If you think the Cro-Magnon look is adorable."

I gave him a stare that could scald.

Edmée held the baby in her arms. She peered at him and laughed. "I've never seen so much hair on a child! But that's good! He'll never go bald!"

He'll never find a hairstylist, either, who will know how to cut his hair, I thought to myself.

I asked to carry the baby. He was awake and looking at the world with eyes wide open and focused, trying to take everything in. As soon as he was in my arms my heart seemed to melt inside of me. The realization came to me with new strength: I had helped make this little person. He was part of me. He and I were bound together with ties that no one could tear asunder.

"Wow!" I said out loud, just that one abrupt exclamation. My professorial verbosity was reduced to a single interjection. As I studied the tiny but potent Richard Beau Ralph, I knew that whatever plans Edmée and Ralph would come up with, there would have to be room somewhere in them for me, and for Bo.

There was no way I would be able to tear myself away from this child.

After all, he was my son. He deserved to have some support from his biological father. Even though he was not conceived in the usual ways, nobody could say that I wasn't the father.

I gave him back to Edmée with reluctance since I had to go back to the university. Bo, the lucky son of a gun, could just stay on at the hospital to do his rounds. He would take Edmée and the baby home after he had seen his patients.

In the car on the expressway just south of the airport, I felt that my car would take off like the planes parallel to me. I felt light, the heaviness of the previous months having been magically excised. I felt so light that I saw myself lose ties with the material, and I felt insubstantial, ethereal. 'Happiness is ebullient for I'm boiling away,' I thought. 'Happiness is buoyant for I'm floating away. Happiness is effervescent…' Well, I didn't know the etymology of effervescent, but I knew that I was high on happiness.

I didn't know whether to laugh or cry, so I did both, sequentially and then simultaneously.

I have a son, I kept thinking. I have a son! How did this happen? I have a son!

There had never been such a plan in my future. But it had happened! And look at the way it happened!

Traffic brought me down to reality. I needed to concentrate, now more than ever. I had a son, and that son would be needing me for a long time.

That evening when I returned home, Edmée was in her room with the baby and Bo was waiting for me in the living room. I knew instantly that something was wrong. He didn't keep me waiting.

"We received word this afternoon from France: Ralph is gone."

"Wh...what?" I stammered. "What are you saying?"

"Edmée's parents called to say that Ralph passed away today. They said he had been losing weight and he had developed bedsores. Rick, sometimes patients like that develop infections from their bedsores, or pneumonia. They're debilitated, so anything that to a healthy patient would not be much of a problem, to them it's fatal."

My immediate thoughts were of Edmée and the baby, but then I thought of Ralph. I went into a frenzy fed by adrenaline and walked around the room like a madman, hitting my head with my palm as I paced. "Why isn't he coming out? Didn't he hear? He can't be asleep! Doesn't he hear us? Why doesn't he come up?" I looked at Bo. "Where is he?" I asked.

Edmée came into the living room. I ran to her and hugged her. "Call him," she said.

"I've tried! I don't know where he is!" I answered. "I can't just go looking for him!" I said, tapping my head with my fist in frustration. "I don't know where he goes!"

"Call him," she repeated.

"He doesn't always come just because I call. He could be asleep. He's wherever he goes when he's not with me. I don't… I don't know where he is."

"Then go to sleep!" said Edmée. "Maybe he will come that way!"

"Yes, yes, I must go to sleep," I said, but I was distracted, trying to think of the last time I had heard from Ralph. Was it this afternoon at the university? Was it this morning at the hospital? I realized that with all the excitement and nervousness I had gone through at the hospital I didn't even register that Ralph hadn't been with me. Then I had to rush to the university because I had a full schedule. In hindsight, I realized I should have stayed at the hospital and called for my department to get subs for me. I couldn't think… When was the last time I had heard Ralph's voice?

"Edmée," I asked. "When did you last speak to Ralph?"

"Last night. You came into my bedroom but it was Ralph who talked to me. He didn't stay long because I was too tired. He said that he couldn't wait to see the baby, that I was making him so happy. I slept for a few hours, then the cramps started at dawn. You didn't hear from him last night?"

"No, Edmée. I was asleep while he talked to you, and I remained asleep after he came to my bedroom. Then with all the commotion of this morning, I didn't realize Ralph wasn't with me. I didn't think that strange because there are times when Ralph goes away for hours, sometimes even a couple of days. But you would think he would be there, bright and clear, for the birth of his son. I'm sorry, Edmée, I'm so sorry. I just didn't notice that he wasn't there with me."

Edmée looked at Bo and me through tearful eyes. "Maybe if you try to go to sleep, maybe then he'll come and speak to me."

I jumped on the sofa and closed my eyes. But my body was too on edge and my mind was too alert. I was still trying to remember the last time I had heard from Ralph. I just couldn't remember. I asked for a shot of vodka. It didn't seem to work.

"I have something that might work," said Edmée. She went to her bedroom and came back with our beautiful little baby, fast asleep in his little baby pajamas. She handed him over to me.

A feeling of peace came over me as I looked at that little face. It was tiny and wrinkled. The hair on his head looked like a thatched hut. He looked like a sage little old man with his eyes closed the better to meditate. After a few minutes I felt that I was calm enough to try to go to sleep.

Edmée and Bo told me that I did fall asleep, for a few minutes. Edmée kept calling Ralph's name but nothing happened. Ralph didn't show up. It was Edmée calling for him that woke me up. I woke up and saw them looking at me with expressions of hope, but it was only me waking up. I felt tired and drained. I felt empty and world-weary. Then I began to weep, and Edmée and Bo joined me, and the three of us, with Edmée still holding the baby, huddled together in sorrow and despair.

We decided that Edmée would not be going home for Ralph's funeral. She was extremely depressed and it wasn't a good idea to travel with a newborn. We were all depressed. I was desolate. I have never felt lonelier than those days after Ralph had left me. It came as a surprise, for I had grown accustomed to having a person existing inside with me. I had grown accustomed to our conversations. Even if we disagreed often, our discussions were always lively and, in the end, entertaining. We had true European-style conversations, not this small and lite talk that Americans engage in, usually to talk past each other and not have to come to terms with difficult subjects. Ralph and I had arguments, but since I couldn't kick him out, we had to make peace. I learned a lot with Ralph, not just from the knowledge he had and I didn't, but also about how to deal with other humans. Since we were joined in some cosmic way, we had to deal with each other and, in the end, I believe we became good friends. Hell! We shared his wife! Or rather, I allowed him the possibility of being with his wife by using my body. Out of that came a miraculous little baby whose birth, for some reason or another, marked the end of Ralph's life.

It was a coincidence we could not ignore. Edmée, Bo and I discussed it at length, but we could not come to any conclusion. Edmée had last heard from Ralph around 11 at night. He didn't stay with her long because she was tired, so he came back to my bedroom where Bo was already asleep. I was unaware of all this since I myself had been asleep since 11, in order to give Ralph a chance to be with Edmée. I kept on sleeping until I was awakened in the morning by the exciting news that the baby was coming. After that, all was a flurry of movement and of time racing by.

The last time I remember hearing from Ralph was at school on the preceding afternoon. We discussed some details that I would be giving the literature students about their term papers. As always, he helped me to organize them better and be more precise. I don't even remember if I thanked him for it.

I t wasn't until four evenings later that Bo took me to the office to show me something lying on top of my desk. Because of all the commotion of the baby's birth, followed by the sorrow of Ralph's death, I had not been to my desk in all that time.

On top of my barely contained mess of papers, books and catalogs sprawled on the desk was a sheaf of papers, five regular-sized sheets bent in half to produce an impromptu booklet. On the front cover was written just my name, Rick, in a handwriting that was not mine and which I did not recognize.

I looked up at Bo with a bit of impatience. "You didn't write this. This is not your handwriting."

Bo shook his head. He took the sheaf of papers in my hand and turned it over. There on the back page, all the way at the bottom of the writing, was the name I needed to see: Ralph.

"Ralph wrote this?"

"It seems he did. He must have written it that last night right before he went to sleep. That is, right before he brought your body back to bed."

The full weight of this truth hit me with great force and my hands began to shake.

"Did you read it?" I asked.

"Of course not. It's addressed to you."

Bo pulled the chair out so I could sit down in front of the desk. He placed the papers in my hand and left the room, closing the door softly behind him.

I turned the booklet back to the front page and saw my name written in a bold, heavy script, not very tidy, but legible. I bent back the first page and saw that Ralph had scrawled on it from top to bottom, hardly leaving any empty space. As always with Ralph's communications to me, it was in French.

Here is my translation into English.

It is said that there is no love stronger than the love of self. All other types of love are measured and compared to, and ultimately governed by this love of self which, it is what it is, is known as selfish love. It is the love of self-preservation and egotism and is always there to counterbalance most other types of love. Unconditional love, say maternal love, is rare; conjugal love relies heavily on the self being satisfied first. I must say, however, that the love I feel for you, Rick, you who are neither my son nor my spouse, is about as unconditional as it can get, and it equals in intensity my love of self. Lately, I am having trouble identifying where I end and you begin. This must be what the neo-Platonists meant by kindred spirits, two souls who migrate together and meld, with no thought whatsoever to what each one might lose in the fusion.

The danger of losing myself in you is of no consequence; I was lost before I met you, anyway, and you took me in. You might say that you had no choice in the matter, that somehow my existence was foisted on to yours through mysterious ways in which your volition held no part. Well, the ways might have been mysterious, but I think it was your openness, your tolerance of other ways of thinking and other ways of being, and, finally, your imagination, whose strength towers over the imagination of others—when it exists at all—that enabled my soul to find within yours a sliver of existence in a place of hospitable shelter.

I think I may know how it happened. I wasn't in
Regensburg during my "migration"; you weren't in Miami.
I was in Nonant, with Edmée, staying at her parents' place.
You, too, were on holiday. You were travelling with Bo
through Normandy. I looked up the dates, they coincide.
Somewhere during the duration of our physical proximity
we must have come extremely close to each other. I don't
know, perhaps we even touched. Where that could have
taken place I do not know. Was it at the Bayeux Museum
when we were both studying the tapestry of the Norman
Invasion, peering at the violent images of soldiers pierced
with arrows or butchered with swords? Regiments marching
ineluctably forward, on foot and on horseback, routing the
English in their ambition to dislodge their dominion over
the land and replace them with their own hegemony. Were
we both at the American cemetery in Colleville-sur-Mer?
That, too, is a place of meditation, of highly charged
emotion, as one observes the crosses and the stars of David
as they fill the fields and hills to the horizon. Remember,
the Americans were there to dislodge the Germans, not for
themselves, but so that the French could regain their
country and their freedom. Maybe we could have brushed
past each other as we followed the medieval procession of
steps up the hill of Mont Saint-Michel? Those alleys and
passageways hold the secrets of centuries, where succeeding
generations of monks regretted bitterly that their lives were
dedicated against their will to the dictates and the
dominance of the all-powerful Catholic Church. Like
soldiers in a war, they, too, lost their ability to direct their
own fate. Somewhere in Normandy our lives moved
together, perhaps touched. I don't remember meeting you,

even seeing you, but then, I don't remember having my stroke, either. Perhaps as I flailed from life to death and hovered in no-man's-land, my soul found nearby a being capable of receiving it, holding it, and nurturing it. It is for this chance that you gave me, this extension to my existence, one that I had no right to ask you for, that I thank you with words that in no way do justice to the magnitude of my feelings. My ineffable gratitude knows no physical bounds; neither are there limits to its duration. Other than being inside the womb of my mother, I have never had, and probably never will again attain, this closeness, this inseparability, this intimacy, with any other being.

I have been feeling strange of late. I feel my edges dissipating, my borders effacing, my memories weakening. The perimeter of what used to be me seems to be dissolving, like watercolors stretched thin to the edges of the page, only the page seems to stretch to infinity. I don't know how much longer my integrity will last. I don't know what is happening to the cohesion of my consciousness. There is so much we remain ignorant of. The soul is one of them. We don't know what it is or, indeed, if it is. It may be a figment entirely of our imagination, due to our fear of death. However, my fusion with you, the transference of my consciousness into yours, gives me hope that there is truth in the concept of metempsychosis, of the transmigration of the soul. That it has occurred at different times to different societies is already a factor that must be reckoned with, although I realize that it is an idea far from being universal. Rick, I know that you are an atheist, or at least have been for quite some time, but you must accept that what happened to us cannot be explained by the usual scientific methods. My mind therefore seeks other explanations. The idea of reincarnation, for me, may provide a hypothesis that, while not being verifiable, can stand in for the truth for the moment, our lives being so transitory that we cannot hope to grasp this mystery. If my blathering comes too close for comfort to religion, I apologize to you, Rick. All I know for certain is that you granted me the gift of time. Thanks to you, I had the time to look back on my life, distinguish my successes of which I am proud, but also identify my regrets, of which, unfortunately, there are many. But you gave Edmée and me the magical ability to rectify one of our heaviest of regrets, that of not having had a child. I confess to not knowing how much of that child comes from me and how much of him comes from you, but were he destined to come entirely from you I would not mind, for you and I are kindred spirits. For the time that you and I have been partners in this mystery, it is my privilege to have met and lived with a person such as you. Talk about giving someone their shirt off their back! You have shared your soul from within you. You have given of yourself in a way most people cannot or would not. For these very reasons I am proud to call you friend.

If my intuition is right—and you of course remember the importance that Descartes himself gave to intuition!— my consciousness will cease to exist when my soul migrates once again. I commend to you, my friend, once again, the care of my soul in its new manifestation. After all, he will be your son as well. As for Edmée, I know that you never had made plans for a woman to play such a role in your life, but as the mother of your son, she will never cease to be an important part of your life.

Know that with Bo's help, who invited an attorney friend of his to come visit while I inhabited your body, and since he didn't know me from Adam, nor from you, I had my last will and testament drawn up, and my estate, as humble as it may be, is bequeathed equally to you and Edmée, with the stipulation that an educational fund be set up for our son for his post-graduate studies. As for the rest, I know that you and Edmée, however you decide to run your affairs, will raise our child with kindness and wisdom. In this respect, I have no fears. I just hope that he will not give you much trouble, but when he does, look straight into his eyes and seek your old friend. He will be there and he will recognize you. Of that, I am sure.

Forever your friend,
Theophilus RALPH

I closed the little handmade booklet and placed it on the desk. I left my bedroom in search of Bo and Edmée whom I found in the kitchen engaged in conversation. They became silent as soon as they saw me. I felt two sets of eyes looking into mine, trying to gauge how I felt. I had just lost a best friend, that's how I felt.

I saw Edmée clutching a handmade booklet similar to mine. It was her own missive from Ralph.

"How's the baby?" I asked.

"Fine," she answered. "Sleeping again. He falls asleep every time he gets fed. Just like Ralph. He would feel drowsy if he ate too big a lunch or dinner. That's why he would skip breakfast and have only coffee, so that he wouldn't feel dragged down."

I smiled. "Can I go see him?"

"Of course," she replied. "Go, the bedroom door is open."

I went down the hallway to Edmée's bedroom. Tiny Richard Beau was in his crib fast asleep. I stared at the little human being, looking at his tiny hands and feet, gazing at the little face, trying to recognize any features, any signs that he came from Ralph. I couldn't find any. This was a little Mayan baby, that was clear. I made a note to myself to measure his cranium when he was a bit older, to ascertain a high cephalic index. The Mayans have the roundest heads of any other population group in the world. I chuckled; Ralph's head had been kind of square.

My laughter must have awakened Richard Beau. I couldn't believe that a newborn had the capacity to focus so intently. I looked deep into those twin mirrors of the soul. He held my gaze as I stooped over to pick him up in my arms.

"Ralph, is that you?" I asked.

With our faces inches apart, I stared deeply into my son's eyes with a feeling of overwhelming love. He stared right back at me, focused and intent, if from recognition, I have no idea. That, I certainly could not *know*. Rather I *saw*, in the ineffable gaze of the baby's eyes into mine, like sets of mirrors facing each other, an ageless repetition of images running to infinity. At the same time I *felt* that his soul and mine had been together before and we were on the verge of continuing one more cycle, one more round, one more correspondence in the transmigration of our spirits.

I hugged him tight and walked back into the kitchen where preparations for dinner had begun. I had to fend off the others who wanted to take the baby. I wasn't ready to give him up quite yet.

Lightning Source UK Ltd.
Milton Keynes UK
UKHW012309021220
374527UK00011B/876/J